It was hard thi...

Making the bed had b... unsettling images of the man who would be sleeping here. He'd stretch that long frame out on the bed, between the crisp sheets.... No, Miranda couldn't think of Jared that way.

What she should think of him as was gone. Just one more travelin' man traveling out of Redbud and away from her. The faster she got him well, the faster he'd be away.

"I'll need help to get over to the bed," Jared grumbled.

Miranda held out her hands. But somehow she hadn't anticipated his rising so quickly above her, standing chest to chest while his warm hands still grasped hers. It literally took her breath away.

She couldn't afford to care, Miranda told herself. But her body was sending her an entirely different message....

Dear Reader,

Where's the best place to find love this holiday season? UNDER THE MISTLETOE! This month, Silhouette Romance brings you a special collection of stories filled with spirited romance and holiday cheer.

'Tis the season for Christmas wishes, and nine-year-old Danny Morgan has a tall order. He wants to reunite his divorced parents. Will FABULOUS FATHER Luke Morgan be able to win ex-wife Sherri Morgan's love—and fulfill his son's dreams? Find out in Carla Cassidy's heartwarming romance, *Anything for Danny*.

Helen R. Myers brings us a wonderful romance about the power of true love. *To Wed at Christmas* is David Shepherd and Harmony Martin's wish—though their feuding families struggle to keep them apart.

Linda Varner continues the trilogy, MR. RIGHT, INC. with *Believing in Miracles*. Falling in love again may be out of the question for single dad Andy Fulbright. But when he meets Honey Truman, *marriage* isn't....

Look for more love and cheer with a charming book from Toni Collins. *Miss Scrooge* may not have much Christmas spirit, but it's nothing that a holiday with sexy Gabe Wheeler can't cure. Lucinda Lambert is running from danger when she finds protection and love in the arms of *A Cowboy for Christmas*. Look for this emotional romance by Stella Bagwell. And Lynn Bulock rounds out the month with the delightful *Surprise Package*.

Wishing you a happy holiday and wonderful New Year!

Anne Canadeo
Senior Editor

Please address questions and book requests to:
Silhouette Reader Service
U.S.: 3010 Walden Ave., P.O. Box 1325, Buffalo, NY 14269
Canadian: P.O. Box 609, Fort Erie, Ont. L2A 5X3

SURPRISE PACKAGE

Lynn Bulock

Silhouette
R O M A N C E™
Published by Silhouette Books
America's Publisher of Contemporary Romance

To Joe, always.

And to Eileen, Karyn and Sally,
who held my hand and listened.

 SILHOUETTE BOOKS

ISBN 0-373-19053-0

SUPRISE PACKAGE

This edition published by arrangement with Harlequin Enterprises B.V.

® and TM are trademarks of Harlequin Enterprises B.V., used under license. Trademarks indicated with ® are registered in the United States Patent and Trademark Office, the Canadian Trade Marks Office and in other countries.

Printed in U.S.A.

LYNN BULOCK

has been writing since the age of ten, and getting paid to write for more than a decade. She is the author of eight contemporary romance novels and many short stories for adults and children. She lives with her husband, two sons and a growing menagerie outside of St. Louis, Missouri.

What to do when you find a sexy man under your Christmas tree:

☐ *1. Check for a pulse.*

☐ *2. Check for a wedding ring.*

☐ *3. Shake him up to see what's inside.*

☐ *4. Take him in and unwrap him.*

☐ *5. Don't let him get away.*

Chapter One

Miranda Dalton was flung out of a sound sleep by so many noises at once, she wasn't able to sort them out. There was something that roared and crunched and made her pop out of her nest of quilts and swing her sock-covered feet onto the icy floor. By the time she was upright, there was the hissing of sleet on the windows, and screams mixed with footsteps outside, and someone pounding on the door.

"C'mon, Miss Randi, wake up," one of the voices yelled, still pounding on the door.

"Oh, LoveAnne, calm down," the other voice said. "Besides, Randi sleeps all the way down the hall. I told you, we should go bang on her window."

"Well, which one is that, Loralee? For all we know we could be banging on the boys' bathroom while that poor man bleeds to death."

Randi fumbled with the ancient lock and pulled the door open, causing two wet, panicky teenagers to burst inside. "Who's going to bleed to death, LoveAnne? And what are you two doing out this late anyway?"

"Oh, Miss Randi, you've got to come. Some man on a motorcycle just missed the bend on Hill Street and...well, see for yourself," LoveAnne Kimball said, actually wringing her hands, which ruined the effect of her carefully applied lavender polish.

With the door flung wide, Randi could see. Her Christmas tree—or what was left of it. And here she'd been so proud of herself, using a break in the weather to get the silly thing decorated and lit today. There it was, the one outdoor decoration in all of Redbud, sheared off with the ground. The pathetic ruins seemed to be covering a motorcycle and its rider.

"He's not moving," LoveAnne said.

"He really isn't," Loralee, usually the more practical of the two, added, swiping some of the mascara off her puddled face. "And we weren't out running around, just walking home from Sunday-night prayer meeting."

On any other occasion Randi would have launched into her prepared lecture number forty-seven on hanging out downtown late at night. She knew that prayer meeting had let out more than two hours ago, but tonight she didn't have time for a lecture.

Randi went back to her room and pulled on the pair of jeans she'd tossed over the chair. Then she worked a heavy hooded sweatshirt over her nightshirt and slid into shoes. LoveAnne had followed her inside, and she looked panicky.

"LoveAnne, go into the office and get Doc Carter on the phone. Tell her to come here." Randi hastily grabbed a towel and headed for the door.

The wind nearly pulled the front door out of her hand when she went back into the cold darkness. Pulling the door shut behind her, she faced the stinging sleet.

One strand of her hair escaped the hood of her sweatshirt and she turned around to tuck it back in before it got ice coated. The sign was still over the door; at least the biker hadn't knocked *that* down. A Caring Place, the bright letters proclaimed. The former Redbud Elementary School was the only community center and shelter for fifty miles. At first, all those years ago, Randi had planned to name it A Woman's Place, but she figured that half the redneck males in the county wouldn't get the joke. Right now Randi knew that this woman's place was back in her nest of warm quilts, but that wasn't to be. She had to go rescue a biker who probably didn't want to be rescued.

Randi slithered off the icy steps, and walked gingerly into the yard, where Loralee was kneeling by the fallen biker, looking anxious. Randi prayed that the cyclist had been wearing a helmet. Otherwise she'd have a grim task ahead of her. The ruined tree filled the icy air with the scent of pine. The pretty aroma seemed so incongruous with the disaster in front of her. Pine should mean lights and tinsel, not mayhem.

She sized up the massive tree, wondering if she and Loralee could lift it. They'd have to. The frozen rain still slashed at her cheeks, sticking in her eyelashes and her bangs. She had to be crazy, rescuing a stranger foolish enough to ride in this kind of weather.

Then she saw it. A pale hand in a dark jacket, splayed out on the ground only feet from her. Whoever he was, he wasn't moving. Working her way around the tree, Randi found his head. A black helmet was still in place.

Maybe he wasn't dead, anyway. "Loralee, help me move this thing," she yelled into the icy darkness.

There was a slithering and slipping and a high shriek. In a moment Loralee was beside her. "Damn, Randi. My grandma would say that was slicker'n greased owl—"

"I know what she'd say, Loralee," Randi cut her off. "Now help me lift this tree."

"Just the two of us?"

Randi's hair was freezing all over now. "You have any better ideas? I don't want to wait for Doc and it would be too long for the paramedics from Park Hills. Let's do it."

She reached into the frozen branches of the pine tree. Needles poked at her as she tried to find a firm grip on a large enough branch to haul the tree off the immobile stranger. The few ornaments that hadn't already been trashed fell to the ground with sickening little crunches. "Okay, Loralee, on three." Randi gave the count and they both heaved.

There was a crash and a tinkle and the tree fell to one side, exposing the inert body of the cyclist.

Randi knew that moving an accident victim could harm him, but leaving him out in this sleet would probably kill him, so she didn't have much choice. He moaned when they turned him over, which Randi took for a good sign. But he still didn't come to consciousness.

"Lord, Randi," Loralee said breathlessly, the stranger's hand still draped over her blue-jeaned leg. "How're we gonna get him inside?"

"I honestly don't know," Randi admitted. Seeing the man even in the poor light out in the yard was doing things to her insides. It wasn't just pity, either. She had plenty of that for the dark-haired, bearded stranger. He was muddy from his skid and blood covered his forehead. But there was another emotion she couldn't even give a name to that shot through her, made her want to reach out to him.

Randi told herself it couldn't be as bad as it looked. The cold rain and sleet were spreading the blood. But he looked so helpless, and he still wasn't moving. Randi crouched down nearer to the stranger. The sleet had slowed down some. She wiped the stranger's face gently with the towel she'd brought out with her. Some of the blood and dirt came away and she could see that the cut was not going to make him bleed to death, just cause him pain and inconvenience. She began feeling his cold neck. He was breathing and had a strong pulse.

It had to be renewed hope and optimism that made her heart leap like this, not touching his sleet-cooled skin. Randi shook off her fluttery feelings and began examining the long arms encased in the black jacket. No obvious broken bones so far.

"Is he going to be all right?" Loralee asked.

Randi shook her head. "Can't tell you that, either. But he's breathing, and so far nothing is broken," she said as she kept checking. He moaned again when she got to his spine.

"'M alright," he muttered as his eyes fluttered open briefly.

"Well, if you're all right, then help us get you inside, mister," Randi said loudly. That roused him a little bit and he heaved up into a sitting position. Something in the effort of doing that took all the strength he had. His heavy, helmeted head sagged forward and Randi caught him again.

"Oh, no, you don't," she said sharply. "It's cold and wet out here and we need to get you inside. Come on and move."

Crossing the yard was awful. The two steps to the front door were almost their undoing. The man's heavy boots skittered out from under his wobbly legs more than once. "Where'll we put him once we get inside?" Loralee asked. "If we get inside," she amended as they all nearly went down the steps backward again.

"We'll get him inside this time, Loralee," Randi said through gritted teeth. "Then we'll put him in the first room on the right. It's got cots set up and nobody's here tonight but me."

She was never sure how the three of them got up to the top of the stairs. All she knew was that afterward her hands were scratched, the right knee of her jeans was ripped and the sleet that was still falling stung her everywhere. Loralee was breathing so hard that every exhalation sounded like a wheeze.

It had been a quiet night at the abandoned school. Often, there was someone else in the building: a clinic patient sent by the doctor, or a woman or girl with no other shelter. But for the last week Randi had had the building to herself. That was obviously over for a while. The stranger's deadweight between them again seemed to signal that although he hadn't broken any major bones in his tumble, he wasn't well-off.

Loralee and Randi wrestled his long form onto a cot. One hand trailed onto the linoleum floor, dripping cold moisture. Randi sank onto the floor beside the cot, grateful to be inside.

"Lord-ee, Miss Randi, you look awful," LoveAnne said from the doorway. "And he looks worse, don't he? Doc Carter said she'd be here soon as she got dressed."

"That ought to be about ten minutes," Randi said, figuring from experience. "Of course we have to allow for the sleet. You two go into the kitchen and get me a dishpan of warm water and the detergent, and a couple more towels.''

The stranger was cold and wet and filthy. Randi pushed off the sodden hood of her sweatshirt, then, shivering, drew the whole garment over her head and dropped it in a damp heap on the floor. The thin nightshirt underneath showed her puckered nipples in the cold room, but this man wasn't going to wake up for a while to notice and she was too cold and wet to want the clammy sweatshirt on. She surveyed the still outsider, wondering where to start.

First she worked the fastenings and drew off the helmet that had probably saved his life. Off, it loosed a wealth of dark hair that was too wet to reveal much about its natural color and texture. Waves of it fell against his wounded forehead and Randi pushed it away from the still-bleeding cut. Under the dirt, he had an interesting face above his dark beard.

His forehead was broad and his nose chiseled. His skin was pale where he wasn't bleeding, making him look like a cool, perfect, marble statue. Randi thought about touching him once but drew her hand back rapidly. What did she care if this unnamed man had hurt himself? She'd been hurt plenty herself. She couldn't care about this stranger's hurts, except the ones she would help Doc Carter fix before they sent him back on his way.

He sighed a little in his sleep or unconsciousness when she drew off the heavy black leather boots. The socks underneath would have to be burned, they were so awful. She wondered how long he'd been wearing these clothes. The black jeans were worn through in several places and whitened in others through the grime that covered them from his fall.

She thought about struggling with the heavy leather jacket, and decided in the end to wait until the doctor got there and they could use the combined resources of all four women. It might take that to prop the broad-chested man up and get the wet jacket off. Besides, she was reluctant to cause him pain. The same inner messages that warned her she shouldn't care for him told her that this man had been hurt plenty.

If he didn't look so pathetic, she would have hurt him worse. "You ruined my Christmas tree. Their Christmas tree," she muttered over the stranger. "Only lousy tree in town with lights, and you smash it flat."

There was a rectangular lump in his left front pocket and Randi fished in to see if it was a wallet. She felt funny, digging around in a strange man's pants pocket, but she wanted to find out who he was. The object was a wallet. Battered brown leather, it held three dollars and a Texas driver's license.

"Well, Jared E. Tarkett, you're in a bundle of trouble," she muttered to the still form. "And you'll probably never thank me for getting you out of any of it." Smoothing his hair off his wounded forehead again, Randi wondered why that seemed to matter less than usual.

He didn't thank her, at least not that night. Doc Carter got there in about twenty minutes and Randi tried to send the girls home. Maudie Carter stopped that idea cold. "Don't you send those little gals anywhere. I nearly broke my neck just getting here from two streets over," she warned. "Make 'em call home and tell their parents you're going to keep them here."

"I will," Randi promised, already shooing them toward the phone in the office. "Come back when you're done calling."

The girls both nodded, then turned to each other to discuss what had to be the most interesting thing that had happened to them in weeks. Randi turned back to Doc Carter. "So? Why isn't he waking up?"

The older woman looked up from her examination. Her wizened face and sparkling eyes making Randi think of a raccoon. "Can't tell yet. Give me time. I don't think it's a concussion that bad. Right off I'd just say exhaustion. And maybe something else."

She poked and prodded the man for a while, raising little response. Even cleaning out the cut on his forehead didn't elicit much more than a muffled curse and one flutter of his eyes, not long enough to tell Randi what color they were. It gave her pause to realize that she wanted to know. "I'm just going to butterfly this," Doc Carter said. "With my skills being what they are in stitching, he'll thank me later."

She taped the wound, making the edges come together. "If he wants to be stitched up later, he'll want a real plastic surgeon," Maudie Carter said. "Any other little hurts he's had have been fixed up well. He's a little chewed up around the edges. Scars on his hands, maybe one knife nick on the right one. Everything looks pretty recent."

So he hadn't led a real hard life, Randi mused. She could have guessed that herself. Under one layer of callus his hands were as fine boned as the rest of him. They weren't hands that had done mining or farming like many of the men from Redbud. This man had spent most of his life inside, being well taken care of.

By now the girls were back from their calls, standing in the doorway. "Loralee, get those wet boots off," Randi told her. "Then both of you come here and help us."

Loralee sat down on a cot and yanked off her boots, which came off with a squelch. "Is he just sleeping?"

"We hope so," Randi said, wishing she knew.

LoveAnne twirled a strand of her hair in her fingers. "Lord-ee, ain't he pretty?"

Randi started to snap at her, but she had to admit LoveAnne was right. Jared Tarkett was pretty. He was a little too thin, tautly stretched skin over his broad cheekbones, but he had a chiseled fineness to his features that made him beautiful in repose.

It was a rough, definitely male beauty, but it was beauty, not handsomeness. *Billy McGuire was beautiful too,* an evil little voice in her head whispered.

No, Billy hadn't been beautiful. He'd been good-looking in a young, arrogant way. But Billy had not been beautiful even in her sixteen-year-old eyes. And anything that resembled beauty had faded fast with close contact.

This man was another story. Randi got the feeling that once upon a time in this man's life, people had turned to look at him on the street. His broad forehead, even marred by the butterfly bandage Doc Carter put on, made her think of Greek statues. As his hair dried, it curled into heavy dark brown waves.

Randi felt a pang of guilt for admiring him while he was asleep. She shook herself out of her reverie. "Don't talk about folks while they can't defend themselves, LoveAnne. You wouldn't like it yourself," she said. "Now come on here and let's get this wet jacket off him."

The girls went to either side of the cot and helped Randi roll the man into a sitting position. He grumbled a little, but that was the extent of his noticing what they were doing, and of his cooperation. The damp leather was hellish to wrestle off him. All four of them were sweating by the time they were finished, and Doc Carter had said things she'd apologized to the young ladies for.

"One cracked rib," she pronounced a few moments later. "And at least an idea of why he's not coming around."

"The fever have anything to do with it?" Randi asked. Now that he was inside, the man was just too hot to suit her.

"Yep. He's got something, maybe even pneumonia," Doc Carter said. "I'm going to shoot him full of antibiotics and a little bit of painkiller and tape that rib. If he doesn't rouse by morning, you call me and we'll try to figure a way to get him to Park Hills to the hospital."

She took care of Tarkett, as Randi had begun to think of him. What he looked like mostly was a starving dog that somebody had kicked out into the weather. His ribs stuck out and he still needed a bath something fierce. Randi sensed that here was another stray in the long line that had come to her door, one that would give her more trouble than any three of the others combined.

Maudie murmured a little to herself. "Interesting," she said.

"What's that?" Randi looked again at the stranger, where Doc Carter was probing his muscled right arm.

"Gunshot, I'd say. Older, over a year, and fairly clean. But definitely a gunshot."

For a moment the knowledge made Randi panicky. Was she harboring a criminal? No, there had to be another reason. She'd seen men who belonged in jail, and those who went. Tarkett didn't look like them.

She stood and studied the girls, who were still sitting on the cot nearest Tarkett's, watching silently and wincing when Doc Carter pushed the needle into him.

"Loralee, LoveAnne," she said. "Come on into the kitchen and we'll make some hot chocolate. Then we'll get you into two of those cots and to sleep."

Neither of them argued with that proposal. They trailed into the kitchen behind Randi, debating whether school would be held on Thursday because of the sleet. "If that feller slipped off the road on Hill Street, just think what the school bus would do on Highway D," Loralee said.

Randi was inclined to agree with her. She added getting up in four hours to listen for school closings on the radio to her already-crowded schedule and then reached into the icebox for milk. Hot chocolate for three and then she would put her aching body to bed.

She ended up slipping into the cot nearest Tarkett once the doctor left and the girls were settled. She had visions of him finally waking to a strange dark place and panicking like the stray dog whose personality she'd assigned to him. He might snap or try to run and neither would be good for him in his condition.

Even though Randi was exhausted, it was hard to settle down and go back to sleep. Who was this man they'd patched up and settled into A Caring Place? He could be a harmless drifter, or he could be running away from something serious. Either way, it probably wasn't good news for her.

The cot sagged and the rough blanket scratched, but Randi was too tired to care. She just huddled in the most comfortable position she could find, listening to the sleet against the windows again until her tired body surrendered to dreamless sleep.

Jared Eden Tarkett IV swam out of the haze of pain and confusion that enveloped his body and wondered what the hell he was doing in a barracks. At least that was what it looked like at first in the weak light coming from one of the windows of the cinder-block room. The only furniture he could make out were cots like the sagging mess he was lying in himself.

He didn't remember finding a shelter to check into last night. That would have been a new low, even for him, but he'd given it serious thought more than once lately. Anyplace where he could get a hot shower and a meal or two and get rid of this virus that had been torturing him.

What he remembered was being on some godforsaken two-lane highway in the dark with the weather getting worse and worse. The cold rain had turned to sleet, and he'd found some Podunk, but there weren't any lights on anyplace, not even at the gas station. Then he'd seen what looked like a Christmas tree up ahead, which got much too close too quickly. Something told him that the sleet and being sick had combined to do him no good.

At least he hadn't screwed himself up permanently. If he had, he would have been in a hospital. Those sights and sounds he remembered all too well. The last time he had experienced that sterile atmosphere, there had been cold nurses in white with looks of pity on their faces. Pain. Loneliness. No, this wasn't a hospital. It was too cluttered and quiet. In a hospital, other sounds would have drowned out the soft breathing he heard from somewhere in the room.

He tried to brace himself on his elbows and look around the room but the resultant pain made him go back to a prone position. Gingerly he explored his chest with his right hand. Tape. Where and how had he gotten the cracked rib, and why did his head hurt? Why was it so hot in here and what was making his mouth feel as if his tongue were wrapped in cotton?

He turned his head to look at the other cots. Two in the far corner were occupied by figures covered by rough mounds of blankets. Holding his head to the left for too long hurt, so he rotated to his right.

In the next cot was a surprise. This wasn't any ordinary shelter. Even he knew enough about them to know that shelters separated the sexes. And the form in the next cot was definitely female.

It was a girl, maybe in her teens or early twenties. Pale brown hair cascaded over one shoulder and onto the pink nightshirt she wore. It was a plain garment, but it didn't do much to hide the fact that there was a spectacular body underneath. Maybe he was having a fever hallucination.

Then she stirred a little and he knew she was real. One slender hand was tucked under her head and one poked out over the edge of the cot. He thought they were the most delicate hands he'd ever seen. It was a shock to suddenly realize that her eyes were open.

"Well, you're awake," she said softly in a musical voice with a little bit of a drawl. It wasn't Texas, or even Arkansas. A little softer, a little more north. Not Kentucky. Where was he, anyway? While he pondered that, the woman swung off her cot and came over to his, hunkering down in a way that made a wisp of that soft hair brush his face as she knelt. As she looked at him critically, he revised his estimate of her age upward. This was no girl. Girls didn't have that kind of knowledge behind gray eyes. And no girl had ever given him the shock he got just from her touch on his body. No, this was a woman.

"You're awful hot," she told him solemnly.

He could have told her that if he'd been able to form the words intelligently. Why else would her soft hand on his forehead feel so cool? "Water," he croaked. It sounded like something out of a bad movie, but that was all he wanted. Cold water.

No, it wasn't all he wanted. Her touch was almost as soothing as a cool drink. Her fingertips traced down from his forehead to rest on his cheek for a moment before they left. "I'll go get you some. Don't you try to get up," she admonished.

He watched her go. There was just enough light for him to see the delicious curve her backside presented in the nightshirt as she turned and hurried out to somewhere else for the water. Pale hair, pale shapeless nightshirt and woolly socks. It wasn't the vision he would have had before of an angel of mercy. But, Lord, did it ever fit now.

Of course he knew it was too good to be true. Wherever he was, this woman was taking care of him because it was her job. He'd heal and she'd push him out the door, or she'd try to reform him. And when she'd fail that caring look in her eyes would change to something else altogether.

She was back in a moment, and for now the caring was still there in her gray eyes and Jared surrendered to it. She lifted his head, helping him drink the cool water that tasted just as good as he'd imagined. "More?" she asked when he'd swallowed a couple of times.

"Yes." Was that his voice? It sounded so cracked and so far away. But she helped him drink again, so it must have been him answering.

Then she was settling him onto the pillow again. Her forehead wrinkled a little above him. "What's your name? I know the Jared Tarkett part because I looked on your driver's license. But it doesn't sound right somehow. What do your friends call you?"

He had to think about that one. Nobody'd called him anything for the past year or so. He hadn't gotten close enough to anybody for them to want to call him by name. The men had just called him "pal" or something, the ones that spoke. And the women... he didn't want to think about those few encounters. "No friends," he muttered. Maybe she'd let him go back to sleep.

"Well, then, what does your mama call you?" Her face showed real concern. For a moment it was so like having a mother again, the cool hands on his forehead, the hovering female presence that he answered.

He started to say something, then stopped. "Let's just leave it at Jared." It was what his mother had called him. She'd stopped when he was nine, when his father let her leave. But that was what his mother had called him.

"Well, okay, Jared, it looks like you're going to make it," his angel of mercy said. "Now excuse me while I go listen for some school closings."

He didn't want her to leave. It felt too good, this being cared for after a long dry spell. If he was honest, the dry spell had lasted more than twenty years. He couldn't just let her leave. When he grabbed her fingers, her forehead wrinkled again in concern. And when he drew that soft sweet palm to his mouth and kissed it once, Jared saw an expression on her face that looked like fear before the dark claimed him again and he slept.

Randi nearly missed the school closing she was listening for in the mental flurry that enveloped her. He'd kissed her hand. The spot still tingled with the touch of his rough lips. Jared was one sick man. He was still feverish and too sluggish to do anything but sleep. But somewhere in his foggy consciousness, he was so grateful for the care he was getting, he kissed her palm.

That, or the drugs Doc Carter had given him were making him goofy. Randi thought that might be closer to the truth. Men in her world never needed rescuing, or at least never admitted to it. And none of them would actually be grateful for the rescue. It had to be the drugs. Later in the morning Jared would wake up more lucid and then he'd be fighting to get out of bed and hollering at all of them about his bike.

Thinking about the bike made Randi realize she'd never done anything to try to salvage it—or her ruined tree. She went out to the front porch briefly and unplugged the lights. There weren't many left that lit anyway.

The motorcycle still lay next to the wrecked tree. Hopefully it would be in better shape than its driver. And with any luck he'd heal in a couple of days with rest and good food and then he'd get on that bike and ride away. Far away. As far away as that bike could put him, Randi wished with a shiver. Because she could tell from the tingle in her palm that refused to go away that Jared Tarkett meant trouble. And right now the last thing Randi Dalton needed was any more of that, especially in the form of a long, tall male.

No, she needed tranquillity. Peace and quiet to do her job healing a hundred small hurts in a dying town. Tranquillity to run her classes on résumé writing and job skills, and time to study for her own refresher class in biology at the community college. Time and money and help to make some kind of holiday season for all these people. She didn't need a man and a motorcycle to complicate her life.

The school closings droned on and Randi snapped off the radio. LoveAnne and Loralee would be up soon, with the appetites of healthy teenagers. She'd better look in the pantry and see what would take a minimum of effort. The nasty weather wasn't going to keep her doors closed just because the rest of the county would be. A Caring Place would be open as usual for anybody who needed Randi and her skills, such as they were.

Randi had learned a long time ago that life didn't hand you what you wanted. You had to fight for everything, and sometimes you didn't get it anyway. Sometimes you got surprises wrapped in beautiful paper that turned out to have nasty things beneath their beautiful exterior. Jared could be another such package under her personal Christmas tree. Except he'd also trashed the tree, she thought wryly.

She shrugged, trying to ease the tightness in her neck. Jared and his motorcycle weren't going to go away immediately. Neither was the coating of ice deposited on everything by the sleet. And the foul weather keeping everyone inside in tight spaces would mean more sick toddlers, more unemployed husbands lashing out at the wives that the weather had forced them to stay home with, more clients for A Caring Place. It made Randi's back ache a little just thinking about all of it.

As if to point out the facts of the situation, a rumpled blond head poked into the office doorway before Randi could get out of her battered office chair. "What's for breakfast?" Loralee asked, her accompanying yawn looking delicate and feline. Another day was starting whether Randi liked it or not.

"I was just about to find out," Randi said, draping her arm around the thin shoulders. "Have you ever made pancakes before?"

Loralee giggled. "Mama doesn't let me cook. She says after the mess Brenda made of her kitchen before she left home, the rest of us are staying out."

"Well, you're about to learn," Randi said. "Lesson one. Grease the skillet first...."

Chapter Two

"Where the hell is my bike?"

Randi looked up from her desk. Jared leaned against the door frame with all the stamina of a man recovering from a three-day bender. His body was slack and his dark hair hung in his eyes. Awake, he wasn't quite as beautiful as he had been asleep, but there was still something about him that made Randi's pulse quicken with both fear and longing.

She stood up, heading toward him. It worried her to see him hanging on to her office doorway. "In the front yard. Right next to my flattened Christmas tree. You really shouldn't be out of bed, you know."

"I wasn't in bed to begin with," he groused. "I was in a cot. One that is ready to collapse under me."

His voice, now that he had more control of it, was of a deep, almost growly timbre. It fit this man perfectly, this man who seemed to be all angles and planes and darkness.

He was still holding up the woodwork. Randi reached him and tried to make her voice soothing, even though it would be more satisfying to strangle him. "Yes, well, everything around here has seen better days," she said. "But none of it's ready to fall down yet. If I promise to find you something more comfortable than that cot, will you go back to bed?"

"Sure. I had to get up anyway."

Judging from the lack of color in his face, Randi judged he was about ready to go back down. She stood next to him, thinking for a moment. She wondered if he would let her help him down the hall. "Let's put you in the old fifth-grade room. There's furniture in there, and I think one of the beds should be long enough for you."

"Old fifth-grade room? So this *is* an old grade school. I wondered why all the...fixtures were so short," he said.

Fixtures. That was a more delicate way of putting it than any other man in Redbud would have. Randi motioned him out into the hall. "Redbud Elementary. Closed down about eight years ago because the town just got too broke to support a school. The kids bus in to a county school now, ten miles away."

"So what is this place now?"

Randi sidled up next to him, trying to act casual as she draped his arm around her and matched his long stride. There was no way to be casual inside about the contact. His arm was heavy, solid and warm. Not fever warm like he'd been in the night, but male warm. She wasn't sure when she'd been this aware of touching another human being.

"We call it A Caring Place," she said, trying to stay calm. "It's a community center, really. We hold classes, run a food pantry—you name it. Doc Carter comes here to treat people." She looked at him speculatively. From this angle his eyelashes looked even longer and darker than they had when he'd been unconscious. "Do you remember Doc Carter from last night?"

"Nope. I don't remember anything from last night after being in one of the nastiest ice storms I've ever seen. It's not exactly traveling weather."

"I expect not," Randi said. "And my lawn decorations can testify to that. At least you were wearing a helmet and riding a sturdy bike. Seemed to be in one piece when we found you last night."

"Who's 'we'?"

He was just full of questions. Randi didn't know whether to be thankful that he was feeling well enough to ask them or to make him shut up. Somehow she sensed that Jared Tarkett wasn't the shutting-up type. He had the demeanor of someone who asked a lot of questions and was used to having them answered. An idea tickled in her brain, but she didn't have time to dwell on it.

"You really have two teenage girls to thank. Love-Anne Kimball and Loralee Spencer are the ones who came and told me about you. Loralee helped me haul you in here and Doc Carter taped up your rib and that cut on your face."

They were halfway down the hall now, abreast with the shelter room. It was a good thing, Randi decided when Jared's hand clasped her shoulder convulsively. She looked up into his face. Jared was looking decidedly paler. "Why don't you just go lie down on that cot and I'll see what kind of shape the fifth-grade room is in."

He nodded and let go. She felt his touch leave her like a parting. Randi stood a moment, making sure he got to the cot and sank down on it. Once he was settled, she traversed the scarred linoleum to the end of the hall. Opening the door, she flicked on the light switch.

Slowly a bank of fluorescent lights came on. Everything would need to be dusted. Nobody had lived in this room for ages, not since Sissy Peterson and her four kids had stayed here last April while her ex-husband was between jail sentences.

The double bed in the corner needed sheets. She went to the bottom drawer of a chest against the wall and got some out, complete with hand-embroidered pillowcases. In a few moments the bed was made, complete with a blanket. She smoothed the nearest pillow, wondering if she needed to add a quilt. The heating system in the old building never worked quite right. She didn't want to think of Jared, still sick, getting chilled.

It was hard thinking of him at all. Making the bed had brought up all kinds of unsettling images of the man who would be sleeping here. He'd stretch that long frame out on the bed, between the crisp sheets. They would look even paler against the hue of his golden skin. No, she couldn't think of Jared this way.

What she should think of him as was gone. Just one more travelin' man traveling out of Redbud and away from her. The faster she got him well, the faster he'd be away. She smoothed a double wedding ring quilt from the wardrobe over the blanket and stood back. The room looked almost homey. She could pull out the cots they'd set up for the Peterson kids, move in a chair. She went to tell the man his room was ready.

He was sitting up on the cot, grimacing a little. "Problems?" she asked.

"Damn thing sags nearly to the floor. I can't get out of it without making my side hurt," he grumbled.

Touching Jared again was going to hurt her. Randi knew it in advance, but she held out her hands. "If I can haul you in here, I can get you out of that cot." She braced her feet wide on the floor, held on to his hands and pulled. She was ready for the twinge of physical pain she knew the motion would cause her back. What she wasn't ready for was the stranger rising so quickly above her, standing chest to chest while his warm hands still grasped hers.

It literally took her breath away. Jared Tarkett was dangerous. He woke feelings in her that hadn't seen the light of day in a decade. Standing this close, she wanted to lean her head back and invite him to kiss her. No, that was silly. He could barely stand, much less make a pass at a crazy woman. She let go of his hands the moment she was sure he was balanced. "Well, your bed's made. It's down the hall here, right across from the boys' room." She turned and walked out the door and down the hall. If she stayed ahead of him, the stranger couldn't see the flush that just touching him had brought to her cheeks.

"There are towels in that bottom drawer," she said, pointing to the chest in his room. "And if you open the door that looks like you're going into the mop closet in the boys' room, there's a bathtub. Let the water run awhile to get hot and lose the rust."

"Is that a hint?" There was the ghost of a smile on his wide mouth, tugging one corner upward.

"More like an order," Randi said. "If you're going to stay here, you're going to do it clean. Are there more clothes that fit you in the panniers of that bike?"

"Should be, if nobody stole them," he grumbled.

"Then there will be. Redbud, Missouri, may be down at the heels, but nobody steals a man's clothes," Randi said.

"Good," he said gruffly. "And Miss..."

"Randi. Randi Dalton," she said, facing him again.

"Yeah, well, Randi, I don't usually look quite this bad. I at least stay clean. But the last few days it's been a little brisk in Kansas to use campground showers."

"I'll bet," she said, wondering why this drifter was defending himself to her. As if she cared. She couldn't afford to care, not about a man. Especially not a beautiful travelin' man like this one. She and this place needed a miracle. And this Jared E. Tarkett was anything but. She turned again to walk out of the room.

"Randi?"

He said her name differently than anybody else ever had. Or maybe it was just her imagination. It didn't have the needy whine some of the clients at the center used. It didn't have the teasing, pleading tone the girls used when they were trying to talk her out of something. And it sure as heck didn't sound like what her family had called her so many years ago. "What, Jared?" She tried to sound tired. Bothered. But the two words came out soft, the way she really felt them.

"That doesn't really fit you. Is it your real name?"

She felt herself stiffen. "I was christened Miranda, but nobody calls me that."

Another faint smile. "Then I just may. I know where to get towels. Where do I find soap?"

"Well, if you don't want to use that awful syrupy stuff in the dispensers in there, I'll have to get some out of the pantry," she said, running her hands down her jeans. "Back in a minute."

She had to go to the other end of the building to get the soap off the shelf in the food pantry, down where the first graders used to learn their alphabet. The shelves lined the room now, some of them full, some of them naggingly empty. But there were plenty of bars of soap, and Randi grabbed one that didn't smell like roses and camelias to bring back to Jared. He didn't look like the floral type.

No, he looked more like scrub oak right now, she thought as she smiled to herself. Maybe cleaned up a little he'd look more like towering pine. The bone structure was there, anyway. She remembered with a little shiver helping Doc tape him up last night. His body was long and lean, maybe too lean right now, but lithe. She hadn't realized until he was standing up on his own power just how long he was. He made her five and a half feet feel like nothing.

Right now he seemed to be long—and long gone. "Jared?" she said, poking her head into his new room. Nothing. She heard water running in the bathroom. He was a fast worker, anyway.

"Uh, Jared?" she called from the doorway. There was a pile of clothes outside the door to the closet where the tub was recessed. Reaching one hand around the doorway, she waggled the soap into the interior of the closet. "Here's your soap."

Strong, warm wet fingers clasped hers and took the bar. The feeling of him made her mouth dry up and her heart do flip-flops in her chest. "Thanks."

"You all right in there? You really shouldn't be getting those bandages wet, you know."

"Tough." His voice rang off the tiled walls. "I feel grungy and gritty everywhere. That doctor of yours can just come over here and reapply his bandages when I'm clean if he really wants them back on."

"Her," Randi said, hoping her voice didn't squeak.

"Her?" He sounded puzzled.

"Her. Doc Carter's first name is Maudie," she said.

"Oh, great. Not only was I out cold last night while two people were poking at me, but they were both women."

Randi stifled giggles. "Well, if you really want to keep count, there were four of us. It took everybody to get that danged jacket off you." Even though it was a perfect opening, Randi held back from asking him about the bullet wound under the jacket.

He groaned. "This is getting worse." She could hear water sloshing around, and a muffled curse.

"Are you okay in there? Because I don't want you drowning in my bathtub," she said, still dancing on the threshold, unwilling to go in, but less willing to think of him sliding under the water in some kind of faint. "Jared?"

There was still no answer. Randi took a deep breath, swallowed once and went into the steamy room. He was under the deep water in the tub, which nearly stopped her heart.

It wasn't just fear that he was passed out that made Randi go cold, then hot. She thought he'd been beautiful in leather and denim. Unclad, he was past beautiful. He had what just might be the most perfect male body she'd ever seen. But that body was also still underwater and she prepared to fish him out when he surfaced, blowing bubbles.

"What the—" he spluttered.

"I thought you were drowning when you didn't answer me," she said, trying to control the panic in her voice. "I thought you passed out or something and..."

He glared at her as effectively as a wet, naked person can glare. "Well, I'm not. I'm just fine, or I would be if I could have a little privacy here."

"What? Oh, sure," she said, slipping out of the room backward and nearly falling over his pile of clothes. "I'll just go check on the bike."

She shot out of the boys' room and into the hall, fanning herself with the tails of her shirt. *Talk about making a fool of yourself thoroughly,* she thought. But it was logical. People who'd been that sick and beaten around passed out sometimes. And passing out in a high-sided old bathtub meant drowning. Anybody could see that.

Anybody could also see the flush that had spread over the entire upper half of her body, Randi thought. Because even half sick and waterlogged, Jared Tarkett was something to behold.

Police Chief Carl Taylor was just leaning the big bike against the front of the building. "Care to explain this?"

"I think it just about explains itself," Randi said. "The owner's inside, banged up but not terminal, cleaning up in the boys' room."

"Drunk?" Carl's eyebrows rose behind the mirrored sunglasses. They were an affectation on anybody in a town this size, but Randi expected it helped him keep his "official police" image. It had to be hard on a man's ego to go from high school football star to police chief in a town so small, you were one-fourth of the force.

"No, just sick. He'll be off in a day or two, though," Randi said hopefully.

Carl looked pointedly at her again. "All this 'sick' and 'wounded' stuff means you're not going to file any charges, right?" Her silence was all the answer he needed. "Call me if he makes any trouble, you hear?"

"Sure will," she said. "And, Carl, you still game to teach that self-defense class?"

A pained look crossed the big man's face. "Haven't you found anybody else?"

"Only Maudie Carter, and her suggestions would be less than helpful," Randi said.

"Call me at the station," he said. "I guess I could do it, long as it isn't on Monday nights. That's Cub Scouts."

The thought of this bear of a man surrounded by a den of little boys made Randi smile. "All right," Randi said. "I will call."

He sighed as he made his way gingerly down the slick steps. "I know you will, Randi. Of that I have no doubts."

She watched him get into his battered patrol car and drive toward the center of town. Once he was out of sight she turned back to the bike and tried the pannier that wasn't leaning against the building. It held clothing, jumbled by the tangle with the tree, but in good shape otherwise.

Once down the hall she put her whole armload on the bed. "Don't you dare put on those filthy clothes," she yelled loudly enough that Jared could hear her through the open doorway into the boys' room. "I've got your stuff."

She went through the pile quickly and found another pair of black jeans, worn but clean, some underwear that looked as if it had been washed with black jeans, and a black turtleneck sweater. "Clean clothes coming in," she called again loudly. "I'm putting them on this first sink, okay, Jared?"

"Fine," he said. "I'll be out in a while."

He sounded a little strained. "You all right in there?" she asked.

"Just great." His voice seemed to come from between clenched teeth. "Yes, sir, just fine. I can't get out of the damned tub, but I'm fine."

"Can't get out of the tub?"

"That's right. Every time I try, this side feels like it's going to—"

"Well, that's what you get for getting in there and taking the tape off," she admonished.

"Lecture all you want. Repeatedly," he said, sounding very tired. "But I'm still stuck."

Randi leaned her forehead against the cold tile of the wall. At least one hundred and sixty-five pounds of virile male stuck in her bathtub. How did she get into fixes like this? This was worse than when the quilting group discovered 1-900 phone numbers.

She tried to think. But all her thought processes kept picturing Jared in that tub the way she'd seen him before. There was that dark triangle of hair on his chest with little droplets of water clinging to it. And his smooth skin, not winter white like she would have expected, but a warm, dark gold.

"This water is getting cold," he complained.

"Well, let it out," she said, still leaning against the wall. Maybe the cold tile would unfog her brain. "Can you get your feet up under you?"

There was some sloshing, and water hit the floor with a splat. "Ouch. Yep. Now what?"

"Now brace yourself as hard as you can against both sides of the tub to take the weight away from your chest and raise up. Slowly," she said, hearing water course off his body. "Okay?"

He gave a deep grunt of pain. "All right. But after sitting down that long, standing up makes me feel . . ."

She didn't let him finish the sentence. Just the thought of his passing out from standing, hitting all those hard tile surfaces, drove Randi into the room. Working fast and trying to be gentle, she curved one arm around him. "Step out of there, then sit on the side."

He swore softly and frequently while leaning on her. She didn't even notice until he was out of the tub that sometime during his predicament Jared had found time to wrap a towel around his waist. That was a relief.

His face above the beard was paling rapidly. "Jared, sit down," she said.

"Can't," he pushed out on expelled breath. "It would hurt too bad. Just get me to my bedroom and I'll sit down there."

They did a fast walk, as fast as his cracked rib and wet feet would allow, through the bathroom and across the frigid hall. They'd gotten to the doorway of his room when a voice surprised them both.

"Lord-ee, Loralee. I said he was pretty last night, but that don't cover the half of it, does it?" The two teenagers stood ten feet down the hall, mouths hanging open as they watched Jared in his skimpy towel. He exploded with a muffled curse, flung Randi's arm off him and slammed the door.

The exit would have been more effective if Randi hadn't known his clothes were still in the bathroom. "I'll talk to you two in my office. Now," she said, trying to sound stern. As they skittered down the hall whispering to each other, she retrieved Jared's clothes.

She knocked softly on his door. "I'm alone," she said. The door opened a crack and she pushed in his clothes. The door closed. Stifling the laughter that threatened to overwhelm her, she headed toward her office, trying as she went to form a lecture she'd never had to give before on respecting male privacy in A Caring Place. Heck, there hadn't ever been a male older than six living in the building before.

Maybe tomorrow, she told herself, things would go back to normal. Maybe he'd eat a meal or two, Doc's antibiotics would work and he would be gone. She pushed her heavy hair off her flushed face. It couldn't be soon enough.

By the time breakfast was over the next day, Randi was too bemused to be polite. "When was the last time you ate before yesterday?" she asked, watching Jared tuck in the last of six biscuits with sausage sandwiched between their buttered halves.

He looked toward the pitted ceiling of the cafeteria. "Yesterday was...?"

"Monday," she reminded. "And you're in the southeastern part of Missouri, if that helps."

He scowled. It was a good thing his scowl was attractive, because it was his habitual look. "I remember where I am."

"Yeah, well, you didn't have a clue yesterday, did you?" she countered. Why did being with this man make her so argumentative? He made her feel like an itchy porcupine just by the way he looked at her.

He reached for a seventh biscuit, spread honey on it and wolfed down half of it. "I concede defeat," he said when he'd swallowed. "Yesterday I didn't know where I was. Not that you were much help. I kept dropping hints and you just kept ignoring them. And I don't remember when I ate last before then, if you don't count coffee. Maybe Friday. I was getting sick and food didn't sound good."

"But riding a motorcycle in a sleet storm, with a fever and an empty stomach, that sounded great," Randi said, standing up from the table.

His answering smile was rueful, but it lit up those glorious dark blue eyes. "So you won't find rocket scientist among my list of occupations."

"I didn't think I would," she said. She was dying to ask what he *did* do, but she managed to refrain. "Are you finally finished eating?"

He looked at the table and peered hopefully into the pitcher that had contained a quart of milk half an hour before. It was nearly empty and he poured himself the last swallow. "I guess so. For now anyway."

Randi would have liked to suggest that he tuck his healing body back into bed and take another nap. But Jared didn't seem to take to coddling. "Then help me clear. Your fever's gone and you can start earning your keep around here. Maybe you can even make enough to pay me back for my Christmas tree. And my socks."

He growled in mock anger as he swung off the bench and grabbed his plate. "I've apologized over that damned tree three times. And you burned my socks."

"They would have walked out to the trash barrel themselves, Jared." She picked up the honey, the tub of margarine and her glass and, balancing it all, headed for the kitchen.

He followed, making Randi think that her stray dog was turning into a just barely tame wolf. Clean and relatively healthy once Doc's massive dose of antibiotics kicked in, he'd done little but eat and sleep for twenty-four hours.

Eat, sleep and talk, she corrected herself. Jared Tarkett was one loquacious soul as long as it was just the two of them.

Randi wondered what made her so favored. He hadn't said two words to Doc when she'd brought over an elastic bandage and rewrapped his ribs. And he sullenly refused to talk to the girls after that incident in the hall yesterday. She found it hard to blame him for that. If she didn't have to talk to those two, there would be whole days going by when she wouldn't.

But Loralee and LoveAnne were what A Caring Place was all about, Randi reminded herself as she wrapped the remaining biscuits in foil. If she kept talking, kept educating and haranguing, there would be an entire generation of Redbud females who would at least graduate high school and start making a life for themselves that was better than their mothers'. They wouldn't be bait for the Billy McGuires of the world.

Jared was in the kitchen again. She could sense him even though he moved quietly. The back of her neck prickled under the heavy hair she'd tied into a ponytail to keep it out of her way. She could stand it no more. "So, now that we've ruled out rocket scientist, what is on the list?" she asked.

"What list?" His voice sounded guarded.

"The list that would tell me what you've done for a living, Jared."

"Not much, at least lately. I've been . . . out of work." There was a long silence that Randi didn't try to fill in. If he wanted to say more, he would. She knew plenty about out-of-work males, thanks to St. Joe Lead and the other mining companies. And none of those men liked talking about what they didn't do.

It was hard to speculate on what he had done for a living. Something inside and relatively clean. Probably not something illegal, she still felt, even with that gunshot wound for evidence otherwise. Whatever it had been had kept him healthy and busy, and used to giving orders. She had suspicions, but nothing definite.

Still, she couldn't have this man healthy and inactive at the center. It went against everything she'd been preaching for years. "Well, then, let's look at things another way. What can you do here?" He seemed surprised when she turned to face him. Randi could see those already wide eyes widen more in thought. "I was serious about earning those socks. You can't lift anything much with that rib. Doc would kill me. I've got at least twenty people coming to Thanksgiving dinner. Want to peel potatoes?"

He gave her a questioning look. "I guess so, if you don't mind a real novice."

So somebody had cooked for him as well as taken care of him. She'd guessed that he hadn't always been a penniless drifter when she'd walked past his room before breakfast. He'd been up an hour but the bed was still unmade. Only folks that came from money automatically assumed that room service or the maid was going to take care of that.

"Find a comfortable chair," she told him. "I'll get you a five-pound bag of potatoes, a knife, a bowl for peelings and a pot full of water to put the finished product in. And go slowly. I don't want you threatening to pass out again."

"That was a fluke," Jared said, pride radiating behind those eyes again.

"Fluke or not, I don't want any repeats," Randi said. "Potato peeling. Can you handle that?"

He looked defensive again and Randi wondered what she'd said this time. "Most of it. It may be a little sloppy. I . . . don't have such great fine motor control."

"That's okay. Any extra work you can do before dinner Thursday will help. I figure you'll stay at least that long?"

Randi found she was holding her breath, hoping he was going to say yes. Yesterday she could hardly wait for this man to get on his bike and leave town. But sometime in the past twenty-four hours, she'd come to enjoy the bantering easiness of him. It was almost like the relationship she'd expected to have with her brother but never managed. Bobby had only been thirteen when she'd left home and they'd never said five civil words to each other.

Jared was, in fact, like no other man she'd ever met. He was just as arrogant as most of them, and took most things for granted. But even while he was being typically male, Randi had to remember those predawn moments yesterday when he'd kissed her hand. No man in Redbud would have done that. No. She'd already told most of them to kiss other portions of her anatomy.

She left him to peeling and went to her office to take care of some of the never-ending phone calls and paperwork. She'd plowed through a good pile by the time he appeared before her. "I put the potatoes in the refrigerator. Is that all you've got for dinner for twenty?"

Now *she* felt defensive. "Most of it isn't in the refrigerator. We'll do fine."

He scowled. "Yeah, I guess. I'm going to walk around outside awhile. You have my wallet?"

"Right here locked in a drawer," she said calmly. "There was only three dollars in it when I took it off you. Just so you don't think anybody stole anything."

He looked a little more humble. "That remark yesterday about somebody stealing stuff. . . well, that was out of line. I guess I'm a city boy."

"I figured that. Country boys don't have hands like yours," she said as she handed over the wallet.

His grip was firm as he took the wallet, then turned her hand over to show the callused spots on her palm. "Guess not. But then, the ladies I'm used to don't have hands like yours, either."

She looked down past her rough palm to the scarred surface of her desk, fighting quick tears and a flash of hurt that confounded her. "Nobody ever said I was a lady." She pulled her hand out of his grasp.

She didn't look up, but went back to the files on her desk. Jared shuffled a little, then moved away. "I'll be back," he said.

Randi struggled to keep her voice calm and even. "Fine. Lunch will be at twelve-thirty. I've got quilters here all afternoon." She wondered what the older gossip mongers of Redbud would see in Jared Tarkett. It would be worth hanging around to find out.

He went out the door and Randi got her mind onto her office work, or at least tried to. So she didn't have a lady's hands. She knew that before Jared came to town. She'd never had a lady's hands, or a lady's attitudes. Ladies didn't have to find their own way in the world when they were seventeen. And ladies certainly didn't keep folks fed and clothed and protected in a dying town, not with their own hands, anyway. No, ladies just wrote checks.

Randi sighed. No, she didn't have a lady's hands. She just wished she knew a few ladies, the kind that wrote those checks. A Caring Place was going to be in the red again this month. Where were those miracles when she needed them? Because that was what it was going to take to pay all the bills.

She found herself staring at her hands again. Darn that Jared Tarkett, anyway.

Chapter Three

Jared's timing was impeccable. Randi heard his heavy boots on the floor just before she was ready to go fix lunch. But the face that appeared in the doorway wasn't the one that had left a couple hours before.

"You got a haircut. And a shave."

His dark hair was still on the long side, but it didn't graze his shoulders anymore. There was no dark fur running along his chin. And what a chin it was. Without the beard and mustache she could see the strong planes of his lower face, the full outline of his lower lip, the cleft that split his chin in such a way that it just invited a fingertip to rest there. If Jared had been beautiful before, Randi didn't have a word for what he was now. The quilters were going to choke on their tea.

Her eyes narrowed. "How did you pay for all this, Jared? Nobody at the barbershop would cut your hair for free."

"When I told the barber I wanted to look respectable instead of like some Hell's Angel, I think he would have paid *me* to trim this hair off and get rid of the beard."

"Ah. That would have been Sal. He's president of the VFW."

"Yeah. I feel real lucky I talked him out of a flattop," Jared said, grinning.

"You seem real lucky all around," Randi said, trying not to let her irritation show. Not only had she latched on to a drifter, but she'd gotten one that could sell feathers to the angels. Now *that* was a miracle, but not the kind she needed. To top it off, he seemed to be perfectly comfortable here. "Even lucky enough to show up just before I put lunch on."

"Let me wash my hands," he said, heading toward the back of the building.

"Do that. And tuck in your shirt. Maudie's eating with us."

Randi imagined she heard him groan. Of the people he'd met so far in Redbud, Maudie Carter seemed to be Jared's least favorite. He'd have to get used to her if he was going to hang around here, she thought, heading to the kitchen to stir the soup.

Lunch was a quiet affair. Maudie had spent the morning with croupy babies and their sleepless mothers and two folks who had fallen on the ice, and she was ill-humored. The only sound for the first few minutes was Jared, inhaling soup. He got up and got himself another bowl quickly.

Randi tried to make conversation. "So, Maudie, what do you think of our chances of getting that new chicken pox vaccine this year?"

"Not in my lifetime. Pass the crackers," the old doctor said stiffly. Jared kept inhaling soup, the click of his spoon on the bowl the only sound in the room.

After a few moments of the deadly silence, Jared pushed his chair back. "I'm going to go take a nap. There might be some stuff coming over here in a while."

Randi felt her hackles rise. "Stuff? What kind of stuff?"

"Some stuff from the hardware store. Disposable plates, and some orange napkins. They're left over from Halloween, and Ted Kimball said we could have them."

Randi rose to clear the table. "Let me get this straight. You introduced yourself to Ted Kimball, acted like you represented this place and talked him out of merchandise?"

He scowled again. It was becoming a familiar expression. "Not exactly like that. He is coming to Thanksgiving dinner, isn't he?"

"Well, yes. But he's never brought anything before." *Even though he could afford it,* Randi added silently, *since we've just about raised his daughter for him.*

"Well, he's coming. And he's supplying the plates. And flatware. And napkins." Jared turned and left. She watched him go across the hall and shut his door.

"Cleaned up pretty good, didn't he?" Maudie said, following him with her eyes. "And if he keeps eating like this, he should put on weight and gather his strength in another couple days. I expect by Saturday or so he'll be gone."

Randi wondered if her impatience showed that plainly. It wasn't impatience, not really. Just a strange sort of ambivalence. One moment she wanted Jared to stay, the next she couldn't have flung him far enough away. "I hope so. It's kind of strange, having somebody else live here."

"That wasn't what you said when the Peterson kids were in and out five dozen times a day," Maudie said. "And when half the grade schoolers got chicken pox at the same time and we put them up on the cots..."

Randi huffed. "I know, I know. I've said more than once that we need a full-time handyman and a nurse."

"And a secretary and a computer system..." Maudie trailed on. "Somehow, missy, I think if you can put up with that handsome devil, you could get all of it. Anybody who can talk Ted Kimball out of all that stuff might get this place back on its feet."

"If I can survive living under the same roof with him," Randi said through clenched teeth. At least she hadn't had to rescue him today. It was a good sign. Perhaps she and Jared could coexist for a few weeks. Long enough to get what she could out of him before Christmas came and the traveling urge became too strong. Randi knew it would then, if not before. They always left. Everybody left. Everybody but her.

Jared Eden Tarkett IV stared up at the cracked ceiling over his bed. She was a kindred spirit, this Miranda. A kindred spirit to the part of himself he'd killed off. Just like that old Jared who would never exist again, she was out to save the world.

He'd never been on the receiving end of it like this. No one had ever fed him for days, made sure he was warm enough at night, worried that he had clean socks. Not without wanting lots in return. Things he could no longer provide even if he wanted to.

With Randi he still couldn't get over the little things. She'd watched over him in the dark of night to make sure he was all right. Gotten him cold water when he was feverish. Given him the pair of men's socks she usually slept in to keep her feet warm in this drafty old building. Randi Dalton was not like most women he knew.

She was going to be so disappointed. When he got back on his motorcycle again, looking for another haven, she'd find out just what saving the world got you. Still, it couldn't be helped. Something always moved him on.

He hated to think of her expression when he left. It would mar the soft perfection he found there already. Pull down the corners of that soft, full mouth, distort the cheeks that were a little too thin but looked so touchable. Harden the glowing gray of her eyes and make him forget that he wanted to plunge both hands into that tail of tan hair and see if it was really as soft and heavy as it looked. No, he wasn't looking forward to that.

His heavy thinking put him to sleep. Noises in the hall woke him. Lots of twittery voices. Great, the quilters had shown up. He'd hoped to stay in his room all afternoon until they left, but he hadn't counted on the fact that he needed a drink of water, and to move around a little.

He went out into the hall, expecting the stares of the women. Most were the same age as Maudie Carter, and Jared knew that she knew—or at least suspected—what he'd done before. It was the reason he tried to avoid her whenever possible. She had to have told somebody, and the quilters looked like likely candidates. Jared figured they'd tell Randi what was going on pretty quickly.

And as they got settled, the quilters said plenty, the old biddies, buzzing with excitement over having a strange man in the place. But the questions he got weren't the ones he'd expected at all.

"Tarkett?" one tiny old woman had quizzed him. "You any kin to those folks over to Sabula? Fella that owns the convenience store?"

Her companion had chided her. "No, Clara, that man in Sabula ain't a Tarkett, he's a Talbot."

"Oh. Guess you aren't any kin then, are you?" Clara said with a smile and disappeared into the room next to his. Stunned by the non sequitur, Jared went for his water.

There was a hum of conversation in the room that had been set up for sewing. When he'd looked in a while later, they were all grouped around a wooden frame, sewing with precise stitches on a rainbow of fabric. He popped his head in and was surprised to see Randi at one end of the frame.

"I'm just filling in for Miz Bailey. Her arthritis kicked in and she isn't here today," Randi explained.

"Arthritis my foot," the woman who'd quizzed Jared before said. "Somebody was getting married on that soap opera of hers and she wanted to watch."

"Anyway, ladies, I expect you all met Jared in the hall," Randi said smoothly. "He's staying with us while his motorcycle gets fixed and his ribs heal. And I'll bet this is the first time he's ever seen anybody quilting."

"You're right," he'd agreed, conscious of all those pale old eyes on him. "What do you do with them, once they're finished?"

"Some of them will be Christmas presents. With the rest we have a big old raffle once a year at the spring festival," Clara said. "Keeps this place going half the time."

"Brings in more money than the state grant," Randi agreed. "This one is a log cabin. The one on your bed is a double wedding ring." She looked so natural, sitting and stitching, that Jared wondered why she didn't do it more often. Before he even finished the thought, he had the answer. Randi Dalton kept this place together, such as it was. And people doing the kind of job she did had little time to sew or chat with their neighbors.

As if to prove him right, she chose that moment to tether her needle and stand up. "Well, speaking of the state grant, I've got paperwork to do in the office. Want me to put a pot of tea on?"

Several of the ladies nodded, and she went past him through the broad doorway, making Jared conscious of the faint lemony scent she left in her wake. "Which story were they having the wedding on?" someone asked as they stitched. Jared made polite goodbyes and left the doorway, still amused that the biggest topic of conversation was television nuptials. One inquisition down. How many more to go?

Randi pushed her hair away from the back of her neck. She twisted it and rummaged in her bureau drawer for pins to afix it to the top of her head. Anything to keep the heavy mass from heating her up more than she already was.

"I can't fix it," Jared growled from her doorway, shirtless. There was a high flush to his cheeks that Randi knew wasn't caused by the ancient furnace going into overdrive. This was anger.

"I didn't expect you to," Randi said, trying to sound reasonable. It beat letting her tongue cleave to the roof of her mouth.

"Yeah, well, what good's a handyman who isn't handy?" he said, glaring down at her. "I mean, if you insist on paying me, I'm supposed to do stuff, right?"

"You're doing plenty," she countered. "And we're hardly paying you enough to fix furnaces. I wouldn't call thirty dollars a week much in the way of money."

"Yeah, well, if you add my room and board in, it's more than I've made in a while," he grumbled.

"What are you waiting for?" she blurted. "I know you're not expecting the law. Carl's already run a check on you."

His eyes narrowed. "You had him do that?"

"No. But knowing Carl, the first thing he did after hauling your bike onto the porch was check you for priors. If you were staying under my roof, he would have checked you out. You're still here, so you're clean. And it doesn't answer my question. What are you waiting for?"

"What do you mean?" Jared didn't look like a stray dog anymore. Good food and rest had turned him into a wolf. A captive wolf not too happy with his captivity, but still tethered by his healing ribs.

"I mean you're like a cat on hot ashes, Jared. Something is bothering you."

He growled again. "Yeah, well, it's the heat. It's unnatural for winter."

"It's just this dumb furnace. It will go back to normal in a day or two," she told his retreating back, trying to act calmer than she felt. The heat was getting to her, too, but it wasn't the furnace. It was the internal heat generated by watching Jared shirtless. Even wrapped in an elastic bandage, he was awesome, as the girls would say.

If it hadn't been so hot in the building, she would have suggested he put his shirt back on just to keep from giving her heart failure. As hot as it was, she was just going to have to suffer the inconvenience, Randi told herself, unable to wipe the resultant grin off her face.

No, evil tempered or not, Jared was good to have around. Maybe it was just having *anybody* around. Maudie and Carl and the rest of her friends in Redbud were good to her. Better than her family had ever been. But they weren't family, and sometimes rattling around the old grade school made Randi ache with loneliness. Since Jared slid into her Christmas tree, she'd been many things, but lonely wasn't one of them.

Having the image of him in her mind, she considered the things she had been. Irritated, exhausted and tormented probably topped the list. Irritated by his attitude, exhausted from her lack of sleep when he'd been sick and her lack of good sleep since he'd been well and haunting her dreams. And tormented. Well, that explained itself.

One look at that broad chest with its golden expanse of muscles above the black jeans brought out feelings in Randi she thought had died and were buried in a very small grave ten years ago. She couldn't care about a man like this. Not so strongly that her breath caught in her throat and it was hard to swallow.

Feelings like this couldn't possibly be brought on by one errant male lifting an arm above his dark, curly hair. He did it gingerly and Randi wondered if the movement pulled on his healing ribs. It may have done that, but it also brought all his muscles out in relief under his golden skin.

He kept on taping those construction-paper turkeys to the wall, the motion teasing just a little more skin at the top of his narrow hips free from his jeans. Watching him made Randi's palms itch with the desire to touch him. She came up behind him, close enough to smell the tangy male scent he emitted while working in the hot building.

It was powerful but not unpleasant, and made Randi's fingers tremble with wanting.

"You could go take a nap, you know. Before everybody comes for dinner. I'll need help then."

"It's only eleven in the morning. I don't need a nap. Besides, you're the one that's been up since five with that stupid turkey."

"We all have to eat," Randi pointed out.

Jared turned, ready for an argument, but then his mouth closed and he got almost a wistful look. "You always smell so good, Randi. Lemony."

"Dried lemon verbena and basil," she said. "I put them in with my sheets. It's an old-timey trick I learned from the quilting ladies." And never had she been so glad for it as in this moment when Jared looked down at her, an obvious hunger in his face.

He leaned down farther, nuzzling the skin of her cheek. "I can smell it on you all the time. On your hair, your skin. It's wonderful."

"Jared? What are we doing?" She tried not to croak the words in her parched throat.

"Standing in a gym. Getting to know each other. Maybe it's the warmth. Maybe I've got an early case of spring fever," he said lazily.

"It's hardly even winter." Randi pulled away. "Stuff like this can get you in trouble."

"If you're a teenager," Jared said.

"Worse if you're not, I suspect," Randi countered.

"You suspect? Don't you know?" He advanced on her, backing Randi into the cool cinder-block wall of the hallway. "I've watched you for days now, Randi. You teach classes and take care of people and do paperwork. Alone. Isn't there a man somewhere to appreciate everything you do around this place? To bury himself in that lemon-scented hair?''

Randi flattened herself against the wall. ''What man would appreciate a place like this? And how could I let him even if he did? I'm telling these girls not to let guys take advantage of them. Showing women how to leave their men if they get abusive or obnoxious. Why would I want to take up with one of them myself and undo everything I'm teaching?''

His smile only moved one corner of his generous mouth upward. ''So it's like the old days here, where the schoolmarm wasn't allowed to have gentlemen callers? Where men were the enemy? I don't think so, Miranda. I think it's time you showed all these girls how a real woman acts. Prove to your clients that there are men out there who don't beat up women or take advantage of them. I think it's time the schoolmarm had a gentleman caller,'' he said, still a foot from her body.

He held himself there and Randi could feel the warmth of him. It radiated through her shirt and pulsed on her skin beneath, forcing a soft whoosh of air through her nostrils. She felt like a deer caught in headlights, unable to move from the sheer force of him bearing down on her.

Then Jared moved closer, just the upper half of his body. Randi felt so tense she was afraid she'd break into pieces. Something in her face made Jared pause a moment, change direction from her mouth. Slowly, deliberately he kissed her forehead, nuzzling a little, then pulled back. His eyes were an amazing dark blue and Randi focused on him, still speechless. ''See now? I'm still a gentleman. I don't want to be, but I am. Satisfied, schoolmarm?''

Randi gathered all her energy to flee. "You know I'm not, Jared," she said before she burst by him without touching. "Not by a long shot. But this will have to do."

The promise of what had been unsaid by both of them hung in the air as she nearly sprinted into the kitchen.

Jared watched her go. What had possessed him to kiss her, even like that? Hell, what he really wanted to do was grab her and *really* kiss her. Taste her, memorize her, so that when he got back on that bike there would be something to remember. Something sweet and poignant like Miranda herself.

Instead, he'd made an utter fool of himself. It wasn't a new experience, he thought, looking at the wall.

He forced himself to go through the motions that should have been automatic by now. Get a lopsided turkey. Make a loop of tape on its back. Stick it to the wall.

Maybe that would keep his brain on track. It sure had derailed in a spectacular fashion just now. What could he possibly be thinking of? He was supposed to be lying low, not staying long in any one place. Figuring out what he wanted to be when he grew up.

Randi's lover. The answer came so quickly and simply, he nearly dropped the tape. No, that couldn't be possible. He'd only known her a handful of days. And who was she, anyway? Just some misguided do-gooder in the back of beyond.

Still, she was entrancing. She burned with a purpose he had never found. When she talked about preventing teenage pregnancies, she seemed to glow. Even the mundane things she did, like shifting all those bags of canned goods into the food pantry, seemed to light her with determination to change the world.

He had been lucky to change the sheets on his bed, Jared thought as he put up the last of the preschoolers' turkeys. Purposeless and as flat as the wall in front of him—that had been his life.

Now he was still drifting in his own neverland. The scenery changed every few days, but nothing else did. It was still a mélange of pointless days and nights that moved him farther from Texas, but no closer to anything that resembled home or security.

Until he'd landed here. Randi had bullied him back to life, fed him, healed him. So what was somebody like Randi doing running a women's center in Nowhere, Missouri? Probably the same thing he was doing on a motorcycle. Nothing, and doing it as fast as possible.

After he'd kissed her, Jared had looked into Randi's eyes. The look she'd given him had stunned him with its familiarity. Here was somebody else running away. Except that she was doing it by staying just where she was, holed up tight.

He wondered what would happen if he really kissed her, the way he wanted to. If she really was the kindred spirit that he recognized, it would scare her silly, Jared told himself. Jared scowled. Where was this line of thinking getting him? And all because of one kiss.

In the kitchen the recipient of the kiss was trying to make sense of things and failing miserably. Randi opened another can of green beans to stir into her casserole. Why did folks always put at least one can of green beans in with their bag for the food pantry? Every church in the whole county brought them canned goods and they were always knee-deep in green beans. At least today they'd help round out the menu.

Jared had kissed her. It was just a brotherly kiss on the forehead...no, who was she kidding? It was a kiss on the forehead, but it wasn't brotherly. There was nothing brotherly about the way his smooth lips had scorched her skin. About the powerful masculinity he radiated. Why her? Even penniless and stranded in such a little place, Jared could do better.

Randi wondered again why he had landed in her care. She didn't really believe in chance anymore. Life left to chance just didn't happen. If you wanted things, you had to work hard for them. And sometimes even then you didn't get them. So why had someone like Jared just landed at A Caring Place and stayed?

It didn't make sense. Things were just too tangled up with Jared and loneliness and work and worry. Like a knotty skein of thread, they were all gnarled up together, too closely to undo without breaking the thread. Sighing, Randi moved on to the cranberry sauce.

An hour later everything that Randi could get ready in advance was done. It was still hot in the building, too hot for comfort. Blowing air out her pouched cheeks, Randi lifted the hem of her sweatshirt and fanned her warm body with it. She was startled by a low wolf whistle that followed the action.

"Jared Tarkett, you are just too quiet," she said, whirling to the sound of the whistle. "How'd you sneak up on me and set up there, anyway?"

He laughed, a low musical sound. Randi stopped dead, realizing that this was the first time she'd heard it. And she wanted to hear it again, often. "I'm quiet on my feet. Any more questions?"

"Dozens. What's the *E* stand for?" she asked, hoping to take him off guard.

She did. He gave her his familiar scowl. "How'd you even find my middle initial?"

"I looked at your driver's license while you were passed out, remember?"

"Only because you told me about it," he admitted. "And you'll just have to be content with *E*."

"Classified information, huh?"

"Correct."

"What if I guess it?"

He shook his head. "Don't bother. You wouldn't."

"Hmm." Randi came a little closer, the hem of her shirt now down where it belonged, the sleeves rolled up. "That means it's not something common like Edward. What about Eugene?"

"Ugh. Even my father wouldn't have been that cruel."

She shivered a little with the way he said that. As if it were a given that his father could be relatively cruel as a matter of course. So they had another thing in common. "Elliot?"

"Nope. Not even close."

"Eric? Edgar? Ebenezer?"

"Not a Viking, don't write spook stories and nobody on this earth is named Ebenezer."

"Yeah? Tell that to Ben who coaches over at the county high school. But be prepared to move quick, 'cause he coaches football and he's mean."

"Okay, so there's one Ebenezer in the county. One's enough."

She leaned against the wall. "Nuts, Jared. Give me a hint."

His eyes sparkled when he looked her way. "No hints. No bribes. Get it yourself."

Randi opened her mouth to say something else and continue teasing him. Jared was opening up to her again and she felt cherished. But before she could get out a coherent thought, the front door banged open. The guests were arriving. Jared's demeanor changed automatically. "I'll go put on a shirt," he said, his voice flat.

For three hours there was little time for Randi to observe Jared. LoveAnne and Ted Kimball were closely followed by Maudie Carter, who was always invited to the center's Thanksgiving dinner because she never cooked anything on any day, much less that one. Two of the quilting ladies came together, and a battered hatchback disgorged Crystal and her kids.

Randi was thankful the ice had melted as she watched Crystal maneuver her unwieldy body around the two small children, handing them each a relish tray to take up the stairs. "Now don't drop them, and hand them to Miss Randi," she cautioned, climbing the stairs herself with that customary roll of a woman in late pregnancy.

Randi could feel Jared behind her and sense his discomfort at the family entering the building. His gaze seemed to linger longest on four-year-old Lindy. The quiet little girl regarded him solemnly, holding out her plate of carrot sticks and olives.

"Thanks," he told her. "I'll go put this in the kitchen." It was the last thing Randi remembered him saying for quite some time.

More guests, all bringing something to salve their pride, trickled in until dinner was nearly on the table. There were twenty-three at final count, mostly women and children. It was a noisy group, and before long, the gym was filled with small kids running and shrieking.

They calmed down quickly once the food was put on the table. Randi was amazed to see Jared being led docilely by Lindy to a place between her and her slightly older brother, Curtis. She was even more amazed when he seemed to spend the meal in avid conversation with two people neither one of whom came up to his belt buckle.

He convinced Curtis to eat something besides just turkey and buttered rolls, and even did the old "airplane in the hangar" trick with a bite or two of Lindy's turkey. He averted major disaster by catching a full glass of milk just as a tiny hand nearly upset it onto the tablecloth.

And if the kids adored him, the quilters couldn't get enough of Jared. Every one made sure he had some little morsel from their covered dish, clucking over him until Randi was sure three men couldn't have put away the food they heaped on his plate. Of course it was empty before he left the table.

The teenagers were set to clearing the dishes while the adults had a cup of coffee. After her hot and hectic morning, Randi savored the chance to sit, even in the chaos.

It didn't last long. "The garbage disposal is backed up," LoveAnne came out to announce. "We put some stuff down it, but it doesn't seem to be doing anything."

"Stuff? Like drain cleaner? That's not good for the garbage disposal, and it could be dangerous, sweetie," Randi said, rising to follow her into the kitchen.

Before she'd gotten any farther than the doorway, LoveAnne was already over the sink again, running more water full blast and switching on the balky garbage disposal. With a roar it came to life, spewing sludge mixed with drain cleaner over LoveAnne.

As the girl shrieked and jumped backward, Jared pushed past Randi. Before she could react, he was dumping cold water on the girl's face, examining it closely, calming her down.

When she watched that movement, all of Randi's questions about him were answered. His arrogance, the expectation that his questions would be answered promptly, it all made sense. When coupled with his intense scowl as he gently touched LoveAnne with deft hands, Randi knew.

"So that's what you did back in Texas, Jared. You were a doctor," she said.

Jared dropped the handkerchief he'd been wiping LoveAnne's face with. "You're right. And my middle name? It's Eden. As in 'garden of,' the place we can never go back to. Sorry I have to be leaving." With that he strode away, and in a moment Randi heard the lock on his door click shut behind him.

Chapter Four

The door to Jared's room was closed. Randi knocked softly. "Jared? It's just me."

"Great. Come in and watch me pack."

She came into the room where Jared was opening up a duffel bag on the bed. "There's no reason to take off. If you don't want anybody to know you are a doctor, I'll make sure nobody tells."

"Was a doctor. And *was* is the operative word there. And not going to be again. Now, before anybody spreads the word, I'll be gone."

Randi stood where she was near the doorway. "The only ones in the kitchen were you and I, LoveAnne and Loralee. They're not telling anybody, Jared. Not that I'm too sure anybody around here would care as much as you think."

His scowl deepened. "Come on, Randi. Why wouldn't they tell?"

"For one thing, because they promised me they wouldn't. And for another, because Redbud has bigger problems than one out-of-work physician," she said, her voice rising. "Haven't you been looking around, Jared? There are people on welfare, or too proud to go on welfare, all over town. Only two stores that aren't package liquor places are still operating in town, because nobody's got the money to shop. Who's going to notice, much less tell?"

She sagged against the door frame, deflated. Jared looked at her with the oddest expression she'd seen him wear. "You're angry."

"You bet I am," Randi said. "Here I've had you hanging cutout turkeys when I could have had you helping Maudie at the clinic. Hell, Jared, she's a seventy-four-year-old woman. Don't you think she could use a little rest?"

His answering laugh wasn't even a cousin to the one she'd heard earlier. This one was hollow and bitter. "Not from me, Miranda. Never again."

"Why? Because somebody shot you?"

"That about sums it up," Jared said, zipping the duffel and heaving it to the floor with a force that Randi knew had to pull on his injured ribs. "What good am I as a doctor? I can't even put my fingers together well enough to sign my name and make it legible."

"And that would keep you from practicing medicine? Couldn't they patch you up any better than that?"

He made a disgusted sound deep in his throat. "Oh, the doctor did a great job. Just one little thing they pointed out to me. Nerves don't always regenerate. Mine aren't going to."

"I'm sorry," she said, meaning it. "How'd a high-powered guy like you get shot, anyway? What little I've heard from you on the subject of home made it sound like an extremely quiet place."

He turned back to her, but with eyes that were dead and flat. She had to force herself not to envelop him in a hug she knew he'd reject. "It was, but that wasn't enough for me. Getting shot was just because of my own stupidity and idealism."

"What on earth are you talking about?" Randi asked from the doorway.

"Treating the children and grandchildren of the same folks, with the same wads of money, that my father and grandpa had treated in Denton, Texas, wasn't enough. I wasn't changing enough of the world. So once a month I did a rotation in a Dallas ER, just to be noble."

"And that's where you got shot?"

"Right. It was always a zoo. One Saturday night while I was setting a kid's arm, another guy came in. He was waving a gun around, stoned out of his mind on something. The security guards grabbed him, but not before he squeezed off one wild shot. One was all it took." It seemed to be enough explanation for him. He moved for the door and Randi blocked it.

"Don't you dare run away again," she said, her fervor surprising her. "If you have to get on that bike and ride for a while, you do it. But, Jared Eden Tarkett, you come back. We've still got things to settle, you and I. Your occupation or lack of it isn't going to change that."

His face was still impassive. "Why should I come back, Miranda?"

"Because you care," she blurted out. "Not about me, perhaps, but about this place. I've seen it. Look at all the things you talked out of folks for dinner today. And the way you cut up Lindy's turkey and told her stories through dinner. You want to be here. Don't leave just because we know who you are."

His hostility hung in the air between them in the silence. "Don't you dare tell me who to care about. Or how. And don't presume that you can tell me to go or stay." His glare was almost lethal.

Randi was taken aback by his anger. "I . . . I'm sorry. I guess I don't have any right to tell you what to do. But, Jared, nobody can run forever. Do you even want to?"

"It keeps me busy."

"There's got to be better ways to keep busy. If I promise not to mention medicine again as one of them, will you at least come back tonight, or tomorrow morning?"

At first Jared stiffened. Then he seemed to relax almost imperceptibly. "Don't wait up for me."

She put a hand on his cold leather jacket, feeling the steel-tense muscles underneath. "I won't. But you leave that duffel bag here. I want to know you're coming back."

He didn't say a word. But the duffel slid to the floor before Jared pushed her aside firmly but gently.

"Jared?" Her call stopped him five steps down the hall. She went after him, fumbling with her necklace as she went. "Here," she said, pulling the chain up from the neck of her sweatshirt. "It's my only spare key to the front door. You take it and you use it when you come back."

His expression was unreadable. But still, Jared's hand closed around the key and the chain puddled in his palm before he turned and strode out the front door. She heard the roar of his cycle. Then she went back to the gym, wondering what she was going to say to her guests about Jared's departure.

He came back sometime after two in the morning. Randi didn't even realize she'd been waiting for him, mostly awake, until she heard the door open and close and the lock click when he set it from inside.

She thought about going out into the hall to talk, but it was a cool night and she was wearing nothing but a nightshirt. And just thinking about having an awake and alert Jared see her in her nightie made her flush. So she let him pass, up the long hall and into his room.

"We'll talk in the morning," she told herself.

She was still telling herself that at 10:00 a.m. when she was knee-deep in planning for the upcoming Christmas party and Jared was nowhere to be found.

She heard him rattling around in the back of the building while the meeting was still going on, but the minute it broke up and she was free, Jared was in his room again, door shut.

She shrugged off his hiding. If she herself had been concealing that big a secret for over a year, maybe she'd want to be a hermit, too. Heck, she was a hermit. That was why each little errand, like a trip to the grocery store in the next town, was such a thrill. She left him a note telling him that was where she'd be and went.

In the hour it took her to drive, get the groceries and drive back, he'd taken off again. No note in return for hers, but at least one powerful message. His door was open and the duffel bag was still on the middle of his bed, stuffed full. Jared wasn't leaving yet, wherever he'd gone.

At least she thought he wasn't. The only nagging doubt was that her spare key was on top of his dresser. "If you expect me to leave this place open, think again, mister," she said to the chill air of the room. "You can just bang on that door."

It was after 3:00 a.m. when Randi was startled out of her room by the pounding.

"Randi? Mi-*ran*-duh?" the angry voice hollered. "Let me in there. Now. It's snowing."

Lord, he was loud. Randi flung the door open, oblivious to the fact that all she had on was her limp pink cotton nightshirt. "You are loud enough to wake the dead, Jared," she scolded.

"Yeah, well, I don't think anybody's dead. I might've frozen to death if you'd left me out there much longer." He pushed past her. "You locked me out."

"You left your key," she countered.

He turned, looking angry and windblown. "Well, you said it was your only spare. And I didn't know how long I'd be gone."

She followed him toward his room. "Where did you go, anyway? There's nothing around here open this time of night, even on Friday."

Jared turned. "Well, earlier I went to the VFW Hall. I considered getting drunk."

"Oh, that's intelligent," Randi said with a huff.

"You'll notice I didn't. Funny thing, nobody in there knew me."

"Why should they? The only one who hangs out in there who's ever seen you is Sal."

His blue eyes drilled into her, making Randi feel the cold of the hallway. "No, nobody knew me. You were right about the girls. They didn't tell."

"Of course they didn't. I told you, if you want to keep your being a doctor secret, it's a secret."

"Ex-doctor. And I do."

"Fine. Go to bed, Jared. It's awfully early in the morning."

He turned his back. "Last I looked, this wasn't a prison. I am free to come and go as I please, am I not?"

"Perfectly," she said to his back. After the door closed, she walked toward her room. "And I am perfectly free to keep my normal routine around here, even when other people come in at three in the morning."

Jared's door flung open at 6:02. It banged against the hallway wall as Randi listened. She heard a string of words, all of them familiar. Then there was some stumbling about, and a moment later the water went on full blast in the boys' room.

There was a howl of outrage and the water shut off. Rapidly. In a few short moments Jared stood in the kitchen, water still coursing from his wet hair and making little runnels down his chest to streak his jeans. "There is no hot water."

"You're right," she said calmly over the Christmas tune that blared over the radio. "I did a couple of loads of sheets early this morning in case we need them for the shelter cots. Guess I used it all up."

"Before six in the morning?" His voice crescendoed higher than she thought possible before he clamped a hand on his temple with a grimace.

"Aren't you feeling well, Jared?"

His answer to that was to yank the radio cord out of the wall and turn around to face her again. "What do you think?"

"I think that folks who hang out in the VFW until midnight and gallivant elsewhere until 3:00 a.m. are not gentlemen," she said, flipping another pancake. "And you had a key."

"We've been through that. Is there any coffee?"

"A whole pot. For people who come to the table dressed," Randi said pointedly.

"Yes, ma'am, Miz Schoolmarm," he said, the smile that crept into his voice penetrating the charged air between them. Randi tried to loosen some of the tension in her shoulders. It had taken her this long to realize she was holding them so tightly, they felt as if they would shatter.

"And, Randi? I'm sorry about that. It won't happen again."

"It certainly won't," she said to his retreating form. "Because next time I'm not going to unlock the door. You can go catting around all night if you want, Jared Eden, but I can also choose not to let you live here if you do."

"Fair enough," he said, still moving. "I think I've gotten it out of my system for a while now, anyway."

Standing in his room, drying his hair, Jared reflected on that statement. He honestly meant it this time. Drinking last night, even the one beer, had not been a satisfying experience. And cruising afterward on the bike had not helped, either.

Not that it had ever been so great. But in the worst places for the past year or so it had helped him obliterate life for a while. Funny, in the middle of a cold Missouri country road he realized he didn't want to obliterate it anymore. Randi probably deserved the credit for that. She had a way of making him think.

His hair was dry enough that it wasn't dripping on his shoulders, so he padded to the old chest of drawers and found a flannel shirt. Pulling it on and buttoning it, he looked around for his shoes. Coffee was sounding better and better. Coffee and another apology to Randi.

"Did it hurt?" Randi asked him across the breakfast table. His puzzled look seemed to take her aback. She set down the coffeepot and seemed a little abashed. "I meant your arm."

He leaned back in his chair. "Not at first. I was too damned surprised. Then it hurt like blazes and bled all over everything. It was mostly the surprise, though."

Randi settled herself down at the table, ready to listen. It touched Jared to know that she was really interested in this. No one had ever asked him quite this question, not this way.

"I mean I was doing this thing out of the goodness of my heart. This wasn't one of my normal wealthy clients who was adding to the good name of the Tarkett Clinic. This was just some little kid who needed help."

"Your one good deed," Randi said, smiling a little lopsidedly.

"Yeah," Jared said. "And you can see how well it ended up. I was just so taken aback by all the commotion and the security guards and everything that they just loaded me on a gurney. Everybody was so quiet and strange. I was halfway to surgery before it started to hurt bad. And by the time I got there, they'd given me enough drugs that I didn't know."

Randi got up and picked up their dishes and calmly walked into the kitchen. "They did a good job, you know. Fixing you."

He waited until she came back. "They did as good a job as they could. I mean, the skin is great." He almost stopped breathing when her warm fingers found the spot. Her touch was a benediction and he leaned into it.

"What you needed fixed they couldn't reach, could they, Jared?" Her words were almost a croon.

"How do you know all this?" he asked, leaning deeper into her touch. It was his turn to hear her still and feel her fingers slip away as his head made contact with her stomach and he rolled his head into the softness of her, just grazing the bottoms of her welcoming breasts.

"Because I've been hurt, too. Not outside where it shows. But deep inside. And I didn't think for the longest time that I'd ever trust anybody again. I didn't want to see anybody, didn't want to be anywhere."

"But you got over it," he murmured, still taking it all in. Her fingers tangled in his hair and he leaned even farther into her.

"Slowly. And only as a gift to someone else," she said. "And only when I stopped running."

"Is this the beginning of the lecture?" he said softly.

"Nope. The end," she said simply, her fingers slipping out of his hair. The moment was ended and her warmth flowed away from him, leaving Jared to feel more alone than he had in over a year.

She was washing the breakfast dishes when he brought his empty cup into the kitchen. "Oh, no, you don't," he said, coming to the sink. "You cooked, so I should be doing that. Leave some division of labor."

Her grin told him that she hadn't gone away for good. "I didn't know if you would be up to it."

"Just barely," he admitted. "How early did you have to get up to use up all the hot water before six, anyway?"

"Five," she said, grinning again. "And I think I might go back to bed. This morning it's my prerogative."

"I'm amazed," Jared said, nudging her away from the sink and putting his hands in the water. "Even you think enough of yourself to give it a rest once in a while, huh?"

"It's the only way I can keep going the rest of the time," she said, watching him wash dishes. She'd never considered it a particularly sexy act before. But then again, she'd never watched Jared do it before.

The suds clung to the dark, glinting hairs on his arms where his flannel sleeves were rolled up. And the movements of his hands under the water put all sorts of muscles into play in his back. Randi had a fleeting desire to go and put her arms around him, lay her cheek against that broad back and stand there. But that back wasn't always going to be there. Better not get used to leaning on it.

She got the idea that he'd made some sort of decision this morning. He didn't look so wary anymore, just slightly aloof. Randi didn't know whether to rejoice or be terrified. The thought of Jared ready to leave at any second was barely tolerable. The thought of him actually staying now that she knew what she did about him scared her witless.

If Jared stayed, she would have to be around him night and day. She would have to face the fact that he was as alluring as he was dangerous. He could make lots of trouble. The kind of trouble she knew only too well.

Randi was doing laundry midmorning, folding socks and towels when Jared caught up with her again. He was bouncing a basketball against the floor. "You game for a little recreation?"

"Sure," she said. "Especially since you found my basketball."

"Is it yours? I just figured it belonged to the center since it was in with the other equipment."

"Well, some of it the center bought and some of it I bought, and we use all of it when we have teen lock-ins...." Randi paused in midfolding, a sock hanging from her fingers. "Now what are we going to do with you the next time we have one of those?"

"I'd know better if I knew what it was," Jared said.

"We take all those teenagers that came over for pumpkin pie Thursday and lock them in here with me and sleeping bags and some big hairy issue to discuss," Randi told him. "How many mamas do you think would let me keep their precious baby girls overnight with you in the building? You, sir, are just what we're trying to avoid."

He almost blushed. "I hadn't thought about it that way," he admitted.

"Well, we'll figure something out," she said. "Maybe you can bunk in with Carl and his son. He'd probably oblige me that far just to have another lock-in."

"Are they that good for the police department?" Jared looked puzzled.

"No, but they're great for the pizza delivery, and he owns half interest," Randi said, laughing. "You can't believe how much food ten or twelve teenage girls can consume when there are no boys around to watch them."

"I've got some idea," Jared said. "Once upon a time I had a sister."

"Don't you anymore?" Randi asked softly.

"Oh, I do. Somewhere. I expect she's still back in Texas with my father if they haven't murdered each other yet. Dad and Edie were never real pleasant to each other."

"While you, on the other hand, were a paragon of virtue." Randi folded her last towel and smoothed it on top of the stack of laundry.

"No. I was just smart enough to get out when the getting was good. He didn't have a clue of what to do with me once I got shot," Jared said simply. "Now, do we have a game here or what? I know it can't be shirts and skins, so what is it?"

"Horse. Or pig," Randi said. "Depends on how much of a glutton for punishment you are."

"Pig," Jared said. "You already know I'm a glutton for all kinds of things."

Everything except common sense, Randi told herself as she headed toward the gym with him. Neither of them had any common sense. If she had even a scrap, she wouldn't be putting herself this close to Jared in an empty building. And if he had any, he wouldn't be asking. But she went to the gym anyway.

He'd already cleared their table from breakfast out of the way and turned on all the lights. Dribbling the ball, Jared surveyed the tattered net at the basket. "You want to go first?"

"Of course," Randi said. "After all, it's my ball."

Fifteen minutes later, Jared was raking his hair out of his eyes and glaring at her. "You didn't tell me you were good."

"You didn't ask. And what else do you think there is to do all winter here? I don't have a television, and the radio only gets about three stations. And two of them are dawn to dusk. I read and I play basketball."

"You must not read much," he said.

"I read plenty," Randi said, stealing the ball from him. He gave a mock growl and tried to steal it back, and the chase was on.

Randi was quicker but Jared's legs were longer. She sank a basket and then sprinted away with the ball again. It was hard not to admit to him just how challenging playing him had been. She hadn't felt this winded since she played junior varsity in high school. But maybe it was better to have him think this was no challenge, she told herself.

While Randi thought, and dodged, Jared was plotting. It showed in the evil gleam in his eyes as he rushed her and nearly snatched the ball. But she was still faster and darted under his outstretched arms.

Then, before she could recover, he had grabbed her. "Foul!" she called.

"Don't hear any whistle," he said, panting and still holding on to her. Without drawing her in toward his body, he knocked the ball free of her grasp and went after it. Randi didn't lunge for fear of hitting his rib cage. He'd been doing so well that she didn't want to remind him he was still healing.

With grace that made her breath even shorter than it was, he leapt and sunk a basket. "I win, Miranda."

"Aw, call me Randi like everybody else," she said, still concentrating on the ball as it plopped to the floor again.

"I don't think so. Randi sounds like a boy's name. And you are definitely no boy."

"Took you this long to figure it out?" she griped, the ball slipping away from her again as he lunged.

"Not exactly. I knew from the minute I woke up. When I saw that shock of hair trailing down your shoulder onto the blanket. No, sir, not a boy at all."

Randi let the ball skitter into a corner without going after it. Jared's voice had changed. The timbre was huskier, the words more fervent.

"I don't know how much longer I'm going to be a gentleman here, Miranda," he said slowly. Even though the ball was gone, he still had one of her hands in his. Randi hadn't moved, either. She told the girls all the time that if a guy started coming on to you, you should move. Change the subject. Anything.

But she wasn't a teenager suffering unwanted attentions in the hallway of the county high school. She felt every inch the woman that Jared saw with his deep blue eyes. Looking into them, she could see for a moment what he saw.

There was a woman reflected in those eyes. A woman who liked having Jared hold her hand, liked the maleness of him that filled her nostrils, liked the warmth that poured off his powerful chest this close to her. A woman who was willing to forget their differences because what bound them together was more important just at the moment.

The woman in Jared's eyes got closer as he leaned his head down toward hers. "Miranda? I'm really not going to be a gentleman here in a minute," he said softly.

"Just be gentle, Jared. A gentle man." And he was.

His head dipped toward hers and those wide, expressive lips closed over hers. Randi wasn't sure where the sound came from, whether it was the pent-up frustration that coursed through her at Jared's touch or whether it was something in him that made that soft moan.

It must have been him because she could feel it under his soft flannel shirt, down where her fingers were tangled in the soft, but coarse hair of his chest. Or maybe they were both making the sound together. His hand was woven deep into her hair and his lips were covering hers, blotting out the rest of the world as they both slipped into a hungry void where there was nothing except themselves.

In the midst of the kiss, in the middle of losing herself in the taste and smell and feel that was all Jared, Randi had a sudden awareness. It had never been like this. Not once. This was not what she'd felt so long ago with Billy McGuire when Becki was conceived. There had been yearning then, and a hot hunger, but it had been a hunger for love that she hadn't gotten. This hunger that Jared was kindling was different. And if anything, it was more dangerous than anything she'd ever felt before.

Even though it made a sob rise in her throat to do so, she lowered her head and broke the embrace. "Jared. We can't. At least I can't."

He slowly untangled his fingers from her disordered hair. "Figured as much. You stopped caring a few seconds before you stopped kissing."

She matched his hot blue gaze. "No, I still haven't stopped caring. But I can't, Jared."

"Who was he?" he asked softly, with feeling.

"He who?" Randi asked, keeping her eyes on the floor.

"The man who killed your dreams? The man who managed to make you believe that some dreams are fruitless? That yours, especially, won't ever blossom. Because I'd like to find him and break him in half."

Randi stared straight ahead for so long Jared wasn't sure she was ever going to speak. "Billy McGuire. The boy I married two days before my seventeenth birthday."

Chapter Five

For several days Randi thought about going to Jared and explaining about Billy. But she always found other things to do instead. There was always a file to work on, a class to teach or to attend, clients to supply from the food pantry, shelves to stock or a meal to cook.

And of course, hanging over her head like a cloud was Christmas. It was December now, time to really get going on things, and it was hard to get the spirit. So Randi tried by throwing herself into work.

She was grateful for each new task because it kept her just a few more feet away from making a fool of herself. How could she explain to this savvy, intense man that she had made a fool of herself as completely as she had at sixteen? And with a boy like Billy McGuire.

He'd been her high school steady for most of four years. They'd married and had a child together. And in the process he had taken her dreams. Of course Randi couldn't put all the blame on him. He'd just taken advantage of her youth and enthusiasm. He'd had the fortitude to stand by her long enough to get married. It was when things got rough that Billy disappeared.

No, there was no good way to explain it all to Jared, she told herself while she processed another client file. Besides, Jared had plenty to keep his hands full these days.

They'd both hurled themselves straight into work Saturday night as if keeping physically active would keep their personal demons at bay. Randi hoped it was working for Jared better than it was for her.

He, at least, had other demons. Not demons exactly, she told herself. More like guardian angels with their halos askew. LoveAnne and Loralee had kept their promise not to tell anyone about their discovery. That hadn't kept them from following Jared from the moment the high school let them out the doors until they had to go home at night. Each and every day they came back to moon and sigh and follow him around.

Randi had teased him when they were alone. "The Chinese say when you save someone's life you're responsible for them."

"I didn't save that girl's life, or even her sight," Jared said with a growl. "I just wish she'd find something more interesting to do."

But she hadn't. Neither of them had, and they were still trotting on Jared's heels like puppies. Right now they were down the hall filling the shelter room with wrapped boxes for Christmas. Jared boxed and wrapped; the girls did tags and bows, which were beyond him.

"Dr. Tarkett?" It was LoveAnne's more tentative, slightly breathy voice. Randi had insisted that they not call Jared by his first name. She wanted to build as much distance into his relationship with the girls as she could, and Jared wasn't objecting.

"What, LoveAnne? And how about Mr. Tarkett, okay?" There might have been the edge of a sigh in his voice. Randi tried not to giggle.

"I thought it was like being a priest," LoveAnne said. "I mean, once they make you a doctor, you can stop practicing, but they don't let you stop being a doctor, do they?"

"Honestly, LoveAnne," Loralee broke in, impatient. "I swear, Mr. Tarkett, sometimes she's just greener than goose droppings in May."

Goose *droppings?* Randi nearly snorted coffee up her nose. Loralee Spencer had actually found a reason to clean up her mouth? Wonders would never cease. She put down her coffee cup. Maybe having Jared around was better than she thought.

Loralee continued, still sounding exasperated. "Of course it was just a job. But wasn't it ever glamorous? I mean, you got to go places with beautiful women and drive a great car...."

"The women weren't beautiful where it counted," Jared said, sending a shiver through Randi. "And the car was a pickup truck. And most of the time I was looking into the orifices of runny-nosed kids. Now, do you ladies have any other questions this afternoon?"

LoveAnne piped up. "So it was just a job? And you didn't get to go anyplace to work?"

"In a clinic with my daddy and sister and a whole bunch of mildly sick people," Jared agreed.

"Okay. Then what about...?" Loralee went on. Randi could tell she was winding up for something involved.

Randi got up from her office desk and stuck her head out the door. Jared's back was to her so she couldn't see the look of frustration she knew he was projecting. "Girls? If you've got enough spare time to follow Jared around, I could sure use some filing help. There are about forty files here that need to be straightened. And the Baptist bus brought a huge bunch of canned goods, too."

Loralee suddenly remembered a pressing engagement at home, and LoveAnne, after a backward glance at Jared, went to the food pantry storage in the old first-grade room. Jared wiped a sleeve across his forehead in a broad gesture.

"Saved. Thanks." He grinned, reminding her more than ever of a wolf. With each day he was also getting less tame.

"They were getting on your nerves," Randi said softly. "And I can't let them torment you to death."

"They weren't tormenting me to death. I just hate to shatter all their illusions," he said. "They're too young to have that happen. At their age, life should contain some mystery and magic."

"Did yours?" Randi asked, wondering why suddenly she wanted to know.

"Plenty of mystery, but none of it was magical," Jared said. "The biggest mystery being why my father seemed to care so much about the grades I got and where I went, but paid absolutely no attention to me when I was around."

His face seemed to shutter. "Not that I was around much by the time I was their age. I graduated high school at sixteen and went straight into premed. Finished that up in record time, went straight to med school and became one of the youngest board-certified general practitioners in Texas." His face looked grim. "Yep, I bought the family line all the way."

Randi waited for him to say something else, but he was silent until he turned away. "I think I'm going to take the bike for a spin. They've finished winterizing it at the garage and I want to make sure all the timing is right."

He put his head down, straightening the pile of wrapped packages without another word, and Randi went back into her office. They were back into their old pattern of advance one step and retreat a country mile. Jared had volunteered a little more about himself, about the real Jared. And now he was going off on that motorcycle again. Randi wondered when he'd come back, and who he'd be then.

She really didn't have time to do more than wonder right now. Like she'd told the girls, there was plenty to do. She went down to the food pantry, where LoveAnne was absentmindedly shelving corn and green beans.

"You're putting the new ones up front, sweetie," Randi said gently.

LoveAnne, flustered, started looking at the cans. "Sorry, Miss Randi. Guess my mind was elsewhere."

"Daydreaming again," Randi said, trying not to grin.

LoveAnne colored a deep pink. "I guess so. Did you say Dr.— uh, Mr. Tarkett was from Denton?"

"I did. That's what he told me." Randi couldn't see where this one was leading.

"Denton isn't a very big place. I mean, it's bigger than Redbud. Anyplace is bigger than Redbud. But it's still small enough that as a doctor in town, he'd know most people."

"He seems to have known just about everyone," Randi said dryly.

"So do you think he would know people like actors, and singers and stuff?"

"If there were any that lived in Denton, Texas," Randi said. LoveAnne didn't go much for the local boys. She was a shy dreamer and tended to spend her time, as Loralee said, "mooning over" movie stars and singers. "Who is it this month?"

LoveAnne sighed. "It's been the same one for six months, Miss Randi. I just can't get him out of my mind. I mean, Dr. Tarkett is cool, but... Do you think he knows Stevie Joe Nash?"

Randi vaguely recognized the name. Stevie Joe was some kind of country-western singer. "It wouldn't surprise me if Dr. Tarkett had at least a passing acquaintance with Stevie Joe or anybody else you're likely to take a shine to from Denton," Randi admitted.

"Do you think it's all right if I ask him for Stevie Joe's address?"

"If you ask nicely. And don't badger him, all right?"

"Sure." She drifted off to shelve tuna. Randi told herself it didn't matter at all if the cans were upside down.

In about an hour, LoveAnne finished shelving, or at least all the shelving she was capable of in her dream state, and wandered off. There was still a lot more shelving to do, thanks to the bounty from the Baptist bus, so Randi went back into the food pantry room and started working.

She dated a few more cans and shelved them, then started on a case of macaroni and cheese. After that there was pancake syrup, and a few precious cans of meat and chili. Randi wrinkled her nose. No diapers again. She'd have to make a trip to the discount store two towns over for a couple of big packs of the things when she went to class at the junior college. Just thinking about another errand made her back ache.

Looking for more items to inventory and shelve, Randi found one more pile in the corner. But when she went over to root through it, there were a few canned goods and LoveAnne's book bag instead.

"I'll have to call her and let her know she left it here," she told herself out loud. LoveAnne would have kittens if she thought she'd lost her schoolwork.

The girl reminded Randi so much of herself at the same age. She was wistful and naive, living in a world made up of her studies and dreams for the future, and very few real people. For Randi, one all-too-real person had tumbled the whole tower of her carefully constructed future. She was determined that LoveAnne's tower would get quite a bit higher. Maybe she'd even manage to turn it into firm footings that would build a solid adult life, Randi told herself. A college education could do a lot for a dreamer. Especially when it didn't have to be taken in tiny little chunks strung out by long stretches of mindless work to pay for it all and survive.

No, LoveAnne was going to keep her dreams and her heroes and finish up high school here in a couple months and go on to Southeast Missouri State like they'd all planned. She could get her teaching credentials, and if she wanted to come back to the lead belt and teach other little kids how to subsist on dreams, that was fine with Randi. But at least she'd get the chance to get out.

Randi ran her fingers over the worn backpack. It was full of books. She wondered if any of them were entertaining. It had been so long since she'd read just for pleasure. Reading was work to better herself and had been for a long time. If she wasn't reading her texts for that brush-up biology class she was taking at the community college, she was reading old issues of the *Journal of American Medicine* Maudie shared with her.

"Lose something in LoveAnne's book bag?"

Jared's deep, teasing voice startled her. Randi scrambled off the floor to stand and face him. Jared's face was flushed from the wind, and his eyes were dancing. It was tempting to push past him, standing there so arrogantly with his helmet dangling from the strap in his fingers.

"I guess it's catching...the daydreaming that usually belongs to the owner," she said.

"Some owner. Set her straight about the 'priest' bit, can't you?"

"Set her straight youself."

"Why? You as confused as she is? I'm not a doctor anymore, Randi. I can't be," he said gravely. "You just can't believe that part, can you, Miranda?"

"Not even after seeing the evidence," she admitted. "I know what you've said, Jared, but it sure doesn't make me understand. I mean, maybe that wasn't the kind of medicine you should be doing. But to walk away from it all..."

"I'll never be able to convince you, will I?"

She was close enough to see the flash in his eyes change from humor to anger. In her own eyes she felt an answering flash. "Never. Jared, you had everything I've ever wanted. I'm never going to have it and you walked away from it all as if it wasn't worth twenty-nine cents."

He looked incredibly sad. "It's not my dream, Miranda. It never was. My life wasn't real. Not to say that I wasn't good at what I did. It just wasn't good for me."

She couldn't resist taking him by the shoulders. "But you've still got the training, Jared. The caring. The skills. So what if you can't do part of it? You could still do ninety-five percent of what Maudie Carter does every day."

He was stiff under her hands. "No, Miranda. *You* could do it. It's your dream. You think I can't see that? Take it if it means that much to you. But don't wish it on me."

She blinked through the haze of anger that surrounded her and looked at Jared hard. His face was set and his hands were clenched. "All right, then, I won't. I'll just wish all the stupid scut work you seem to enjoy around here on you, if that suits you."

His face was impassive. "Oddly enough, it does, Miranda. I'll get to it as soon as I put away my helmet."

"Do that," she told him. "And during dinner you can tell me how you are at filing."

She could almost hear him splutter as she headed for the door.

He wasn't much at filing, Jared discovered. It took only fifteen minutes at a stretch for him to get bored silly by the mindless task. But since that was about eleven minutes more than Randi could spend at it without muttering to herself, he got a good deal accomplished in two days.

It was better when Randi wasn't in the office with him. Then he could concentrate of the filing instead of being aware of her every second. Her heavy hair made noises of its own brushing against her desk chair and the papers on the surface of her desk. And the scent of her filled the little space, especially on the days when the heater was malfunctioning and making the whole building feel like a tropical paradise instead of Missouri in December.

When he made up his mind and headed for the doorway, he was startled to hear her voice. "Don't do it, Tarkett. Don't you go getting on that bike and tooling off.

There will be at least fourteen families coming who need stuff out of the food pantry starting at five, and I need a crew to help bag. You're my crew."

"Aw, hell," he muttered. "Wrap stuff, Jared. File, Jared. Shove stuff into grocery sacks, Jared."

Her gray eyes were sharp on him. "And tell me truthfully you don't like the work."

He couldn't. Each thing he'd done around the center got him going in a new way. "All right, you win. Who else is going to be filling bags?"

"The Redbud Junior Service League."

He groaned then. The JSL was nothing more than a fancy name for the girls who stood at the bus stop in the mornings on the way to the district high school: Love-Anne, Loralee and two of their friends who were even more hopeless and giggly than they were. "I'm doomed."

"It's a challenge, Jared. Embrace the challenge."

"I'd rather embrace the challenger," he countered.

"Get all the bags filled and we'll talk." Jared nearly dropped his last file when he saw the grin and wink that Randi handed out with her flip remark. Maybe there was hope after all, he told himself. Maybe he could get her to play hooky just once.

There were eighteen families who needed groceries. By seven Jared was so tired, he was ready to drop. It wasn't just pushing the ancient grocery cart around and filling up the bags. It was the mental tiredness of thinking about these women.

They all looked a little battered around the edges. There were too many little children clinging to their skirts and worn jeans, and not enough money. It shredded little pieces of him to tell each one that they were out of diapers, or milk, or whatever else they'd asked for.

Now there were three women and about seven little children still waiting in the pickup area, and Jared was setting five sacks of groceries on the table. "Number 502," he called out. Randi had explained the system, which meant that folks didn't have to give their names out to everybody working at the center. That way it was less embarrassing, she'd told him.

Still, he knew this one. It was Crystal from Thanksgiving dinner. He wondered how life could get much more demoralizing for her. She was bone thin, with colorless lank hair, and her T-shirt top stretched out of shape by the bulge in her middle. Another baby, to join the other children rolling in a puppy heap on the floor.

"Curtis, Lindy," she called. "We've got to go now. Come on and help Mama."

The littlest girl bounded up and came over to where Jared was standing. She stood, looking at him, solemn and sober, a grubby thumb in her mouth. She too was too thin, with wispy hair. "Hi, remember me?" Jared asked, trying to ignore the dirt smudges on her face and the fact that she needed a tissue. "I helped you cut your turkey the other day."

She stood silent in front of him for so long, he wondered if she had heard. Or maybe even four-year-olds didn't talk to strangers these days. Then she popped the thumb out with an audible noise. "I remember." She looked at him silently again for a moment and then, reinserting her thumb, turned away.

"A woman of few words," Randi noted behind him. "Two more orders and we're done."

"Then we can collapse," he said gratefully, heading back to the shelves. "Okay, ladies," he called in front of himself to the Junior Service League. "Who wants to load the canned goods while I look for detergent?"

* * *

Randi stood, trying to ease her aching back. Everything hurt tonight. The Junior Service Leaguers had left after voluble goodbyes to Jared and very little to her. Jared himself was stowing the last order in Sarah Jane's van. He should be back through the doorway any old second now, she told herself.

He was. He burst through the kitchen door just about the time Randi heard the motor on the old van chug into life. "Miranda," he said sternly. "We've got trouble. At least the center has trouble. Or a problem to fix. That last woman you had me help—"

"Sarah Jane?" Randi asked.

"If that's her name, yeah. Anyway, when I went out to carry her sacks for her..."

"You found out she lives in her van," Randi finished, watching the skin around his mouth get even paler.

"So what are you going to do about it?" Jared asked, looking almost frantic.

"Nothing," Randi said simply. "There is not one earthly thing I can do about it. Sarah Jane lives in her van because she lost her apartment. She stores her furniture in a friend's basement. And she and Blinky live in the van."

"Blinky?"

"You mean you weren't assaulted by a Chihuahua when you put the sacks in the van?"

"Must have been hiding under a seat," Jared grumbled. "What do you mean there's nothing you can do about it? Can't we get her money? Find her an affordable place?"

"Jared, I'm lucky she'll take food," Randi said.

"But how does she survive?" Jared asked, running a hand through his hair. "How does she cook that food? Or take a bath? Or...anything?"

"She cooks over a camp stove when she parks at night on the Redbud Glassworks parking lot outside of town. And she takes a bath here, or at Maudie's. I haven't ever asked about some of her other problems because Sarah Jane is too proud to tell me how she survives," Randi said. "I just know that I'm doing the best I can for her because this is all she'll take. If I push, she'll disappear, and then she'll be even worse off than she is now."

Jared's eyes narrowed. "You sound like somebody with more experience than I'd want in living in a van."

"I've lived pretty cheaply," Randi said. "Seventeen-year-old newlyweds do not live in palaces. And eighteen-year-old divorcées live even worse." She closed her mouth, shocked that she'd shared what so few people knew. Jared stayed silent. "You're obviously as tired as I am, Jared. Why don't we call it a night?"

"Why don't we?" He seemed to perk up a little. "What kind of night shall we call it?"

"One to recuperate," Randi told him. "Tomorrow's Doc's clinic day for the Head Start program kids in the county and that minibus of preschoolers who all think they're getting shots will show up mighty early."

Jared winced. "I'm sure it will." He rolled his shoulders in a way that made all of his chest muscles ripple under his shirt. Randi was still just as tired, but at least now she was entertained. "Want to conserve water and shower together?"

"Not likely, Jared Eden," she said. "You just head it on to the boys' room and I'll go to the girls'." Randi tried to toss her head in preparation for a smart remark and regretted it instantly. She couldn't stifle the gasp that her aching back muscles produced.

"You have back problems, don't you?" Jared said. "Every time you do something heavy, you come up tender."

"How can you tell?" Randi thought she hid it pretty well. Only Maudie had ever noticed.

"You cock one hip higher than the other and favor that leg," Jared said. Trust a former physician to look at her whole body like a machine. Randi felt more self-conscious than ever.

"Well, you're right," she said. "I've had back problems ever since . . . well, for a long time. Since high school."

"Tell me he didn't hit you." Jared's voice was so grim, it spun Randi around.

"Never," she reassured him. "We had our problems, but they were never that kind, I promise." He relaxed, grudgingly. "The back pain's not a big thing, anyway," she said. "I'll soak for a while in the tub and be fine."

"You'd be better if you let me work on you a while," Jared said. "I may not have a lot of fine motor control, but I bet I can still give a mean massage."

"I'll bet you can," Randi said, unable to suppress a grin. "The way I feel tonight, I'm almost game to let you try."

"Forget almost," Jared said. "We'll both shower and I'll meet you in your room in twenty minutes, okay?"

"Deal," Randi said. Every muscle in her body ached in time with her back. Together they managed to drown out the shrieking of her good common sense as she contemplated putting herself in Jared's hands.

By the time she finished her shower and was padding back to her room in woolly socks and comfortable sweats, she still wasn't apprehensive enough, she told herself. There they were, all alone in the building, and she was going to let Jared put his hands all over her body. As tired as she was, it didn't sound as threatening as it should have.

He was sitting next to her bed, cross-legged on the floor with a pair of jelly glasses filled with rose-colored liquid. "The last time I went into town I bought a bottle of wine. Can I talk you into indulging? For purely medicinal purposes, of course."

"Of course," she echoed. She settled herself on the bed. That was a generous term for the old vinyl-covered chaise that had been in the nurse's office even when she was a student here. Still, it was long enough and wide enough to hold her and her nest of quilts and pillows, and that was enough. It looked pretty puny with Jared in the room.

"So sip and stretch out, Miranda," he said. "Where does it hurt the most?"

"My lower back," she said. "But it's a pretty normal kind of ache."

"Well, normal or not, we'll work in to there, then." He took one foot in his hand and started kneading her arch in a way that made Randi want to purr. After a few more sips of his wine and feeling his firm muscled hands on her body, she did actually purr.

"Jared, you are really good at this," she said drowsily. "You should give classes here or something. No, scratch that. If we told the world you were giving massage therapy, all the wrong people would sign up."

His laugh was low and had a bitter tinge to it. "And then their mamas would ride you out of town on a rail, wouldn't they, Miranda?"

"Probably. Now why doesn't that disturb me much?" He was working up from her calves to her thighs now. Randi's common sense had been thoroughly drowned by wine and exhaustion. Jared giving her a massage was the most wonderful thing that had happened in years. When he actually got to her lower back, easing the knots out of her muscles expertly, she almost wept with the pleasure of it.

Randi tried to search what little shreds were left of her mind for memories of a more pleasurable experience. When was the last time an adult human being, other than Jared, had touched her in a loving fashion? It was too long ago to think about. Somehow the thought made a tear or two seep out of her closed lids.

He stopped immediately, and his warm breath was on her cheek. "Am I hurting you, Miranda?"

"No, Jared. I'm hurting myself," she said.

"What do you mean?" The roughness of his end-of-the-day beard grazed her cheek.

She sighed, on the verge of real tears. "Oh, Jared. You feel so good. Too good. It's tearing me up inside to know you feel this good, and to know I'm going to have to tell you to stop."

His voice was a breathy growl. "So don't tell me. And I won't stop. We'll just go on from here, Miranda. I won't hurt you, sweetheart. I just want to touch you tonight. To fix with my hands what I can't throw money at, as you so aptly put it. To take care of the lady who's taking care of this whole damned town."

His hands went back to work. "Do you know that last year everything this shelter did only cost $42,000?"

"That's all we had to spend," Randi said drowsily.

"I'm not arguing," Jared said. "I'm trying to compliment you. Hell, Miranda, my part of the Tarkett Clinic malpractice insurance cost more than that."

"Doc works cheap, and there aren't a lot of other costs," she murmured, sinking deeper into the spell of his hands again.

"Yeah, not when the director of the center doesn't take a salary. How are you ever going to go on from here if you don't pay yourself a living wage, Miranda?" he chided, working up to her shoulders.

"Who says I'm going anywhere?" she asked.

"Oh, you could stay here. And right now I'd be real put out if you moved on. But in the long run this isn't enough, is it, Randi? Convince me that you can live and die and be happy at the end of it all without anyone ever calling you 'Dr. Dalton.'"

She shrugged his hands off her shoulders. Suddenly their teasing pressure was too much. "That dream's gone, Jared. I don't know how you know so much about it, but it's not going to happen."

"Not if you don't let it. And why won't you let it, Randi? Every time you and Maudie get going, every time another sick little kid comes in here, you get that yearning look. That look I never had. You were meant to be a doctor."

"Maybe so," she agreed, sitting up to face him. "But somebody a long time ago took care of that for me, Jared. They made me realize that nobody would be better off with a little hick like me as their doctor. I may be book smart, but I'm not smart the way it counts, not when you have someone's life in your hands. I can't do it."

"You already have, babe," he said softly, putting his hands around her face. "My life's been in your hands more than once. And I'd put it there again. And what about Sarah Jane, and Lindy, and LoveAnne and all the others? At least think on it.''

His blue eyes glowed cobalt, and Randi couldn't say the evil things her heart wanted her to shout at him for bringing up the sorest subject in her life. She took a deep breath and let it out instead. ''How about I sleep on it? I'm going to fall over if I don't lie down naturally soon.''

Jared didn't release her head as she'd hoped. Instead he came down slowly, sweetly and kissed her good-night. It was a kiss that promised he'd be there in the morning, a kiss that almost made her invite him to share her too-narrow couch. Almost. The wine was wearing off and Randi's common sense was back.

''Turn out the light on your way out,'' she said to him. He let go of her then, and nodded. He picked up his wineglass, got to the door and doused the light before he spoke again.

''Every school has a Christmas vacation. When's yours, schoolmarm?''

''Soon, I think, Jared. Very soon,'' she said in a voice no louder than a whisper. Then she listened to him close her door and go down the hall to where his wider, but still-empty bed lay before him. And then, once both doors were shut between them, Randi wept.

Silhouette Reader Service™

Dear Reader,

Get out a coin—kiss it for good luck—and go to work on the WIN-A-FORTUNE tickets enclosed. You could end up a million dollars richer!

By returning these tickets you'll also be in the running for hundreds of other cash prizes we'll be giving away. It costs nothing to play this game—there's no fee, and no purchase is necessary!

We're holding this sweepstakes to introduce you to the benefits of the Silhouette Reader Service™. Scratch off the gold boxes on the enclosed Lucky 7 Slot Machine Game and we'll send you free books!

How many FREE BOOKS will you get? Play the Slot Machine Game and see! These books are absolutely free, with no obligation to buy anything!

The Silhouette Reader Service is **not** like some book clubs. We charge you nothing—ZERO—for your first shipment. And you don't have to make any minimum number of purchases—not even one!

over, please

For example, you could accept your FREE BOOKS and cancel immediately, by writing "please cancel" on the shipping statement and returning it to us. You'll owe nothing and be under no further obligation!

But the fact is, thousands of readers enjoy receiving books by mail from the Reader Service. They look forward to getting the best new romance novels each month before they arrive in bookstores. And they like our discount prices!

I'm hoping that after receiving your free books you'll want to remain a subscriber. But the choice is yours—to continue or cancel, any time at all!

Pamela Powers

Pamela Powers for Silhouette

P.S. If you're accepting free books, play the "Ace of Hearts" game for a *free MYSTERY GIFT!*

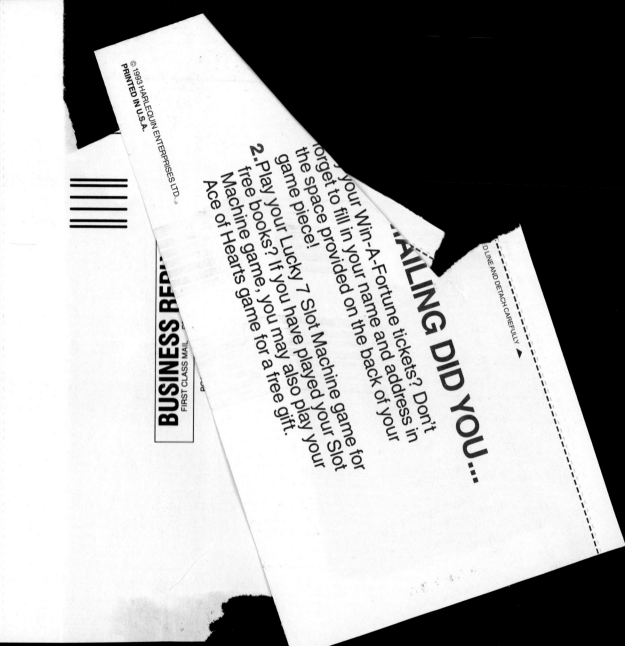

MAILING DID YOU...

...your Win-A-Fortune tickets? Don't forget to fill in your name and address in the space provided on the back of your game piece!

2. Play your Lucky 7 Slot Machine game for free books? If you have played your Slot Machine game, you may also play your Ace of Hearts game for a free gift.

Chapter Six

Jared woke in the morning with the taste of old wine and fatigue lingering in his mouth. It wasn't a pretty combination, and he wondered how Randi did it every morning. She didn't usually have the wine to deal with, but he suspected the fatigue was always with her. How did she drag her body out of bed knowing that it only meant feeding more people, trying to find shelter for more people, attempting to keep one more child's life on track?

He wasn't quite sure as he stood in the middle of the cool floor and stretched. Most of the time he didn't even want to find out. The highest part of the stretch made him wince a little. Maybe he needed to get on the bike for a while and cruise. He definitely needed to do something to work the kinks out.

Once he'd showered and dressed and headed out to the kitchen it was nearly eight-thirty. Randi had probably been up for hours. When he saw that breakfast was cold cereal, he knew she'd been up for hours, and wasn't too happy about being up alone. He ate a bowl of some kind of nutritious flakes that tasted like wallboard and headed to the front of the building.

It was hearing the chuffing stop of the minibus that reminded him what the agenda for the day was. Doc Maudie was in here somewhere ready to puncture a bunch of preschoolers. Maybe nobody would notice if he worked while wearing earplugs. Maybe he'd see if the roof needed fixing. Maybe he'd emigrate to Canada.

The children, several of whom were howling, and their teachers, who looked impossibly young, came in the door just as he passed it. For a moment they were just a swirling mass of humanity. Then Jared picked out a familiar face. "Hey, Lindy," he called to one waif with bright blue moon boots and a too-light jacket over a thin cotton dress.

She stopped wailing and stood in the middle of the hall. Her pale hair was a tangled cloud and one tear coursed crystalline down her cheek, making a track in dirt that Jared knew her mother would not have approved of. By way of a greeting she stuck her thumb in her mouth, shuddered a little and stood still. Jared squatted down to get to her level, instinctively knowing that his height was probably scary to someone who didn't reach his belt buckle.

"You're going to visit Doc Maudie, huh?" he asked softly. Lindy nodded. Her eyes got even bigger and the thumb threatened to come out again.

"Want me to come with you?" Jared didn't know what on earth he could do for her. He couldn't imagine what his reaction was going to be if that woman had to puncture this baby with one of her needles. He prayed she was good. But the fast nod he got in return for his question cinched things. "Then come on," he said, holding out a hand. Impossibly tiny fingers curled around his and held tight.

He stood up, fighting the urge to scoop Lindy up in his arms and run away with her. To protect her the way he couldn't protect Randi, or even himself. But he knew that wasn't his job. If Lindy needed anything right now, it was just a friend. So he squeezed her fingers in return and stood there unrepentant, while the young women got everyone in line. They gave him some odd looks, but he ignored them.

He could feel Randi's gaze before he turned around to verify that she was standing in the office doorway looking at him. "Feel the need for a tuberculin tine test, Jared?"

"As a matter of fact, I haven't had one in a while," he said nonchalantly. "Might as well re-up, I guess."

"Might as well," she said, tilting her head in a way that made sunlight bounce off the gleaming, pale brown mass she'd caught up over one shoulder. "Let me know how it goes."

"You'll be able to hear, I expect," he said, moving forward in the line that was heading for Doc Maudie's door. Beside him Lindy clutched his hand even tighter.

He had to hand it to Maudie Carter, Jared told himself. She might be a curmudgeon with the grown-ups, but she was as gentle as possible with these scared little kids. She didn't lie to them, either. "This is going to prickle some," she told the whole group before she started the first tine test. "Anybody have a kitty at home?"

A couple of hands went up. "Ever squeeze his belly too hard and have him scratch you?"

Most of the hands stayed up. The red-haired little boy in front of Lindy, who had wriggled the whole time, kept on wriggling and added sound to his wriggling. "Mine's a she and she scratches like thunder when you squeeze her," he volunteered.

"Well, Zach, this isn't going to hurt nearly as much as that kitty," Doc Maudie told him. "You gonna let me do it without hollering?"

"I might," he said. "If you've got airplane stickers for after."

"I've got airplanes, unicorns, hearts and bears," she said, motioning toward a basket. "Take your choice after your prickle."

The line moved slowly but resolutely. Nobody was screaming loudly enough to take paint off the walls. Lindy had let go of Jared's hand, and he kept pace with her. It wasn't hard, given the quality of the line.

While he was watching the youngster at the head of the line, he felt the need for conversation. "So, is Lindy short for anything?"

She looked up at him. "I'm not short. Mama says I'm too long for my jeans."

"No, I mean your name. They call you anything at home besides Lindy?"

The thumb popped out again. "B'linda Marie. But only when Mama's mad."

Belinda. *Beautiful.* Chances were good she didn't speak Spanish, Jared thought wryly. By then they were up to Doc Carter in the line. Lindy's thumb went into her mouth as Jared swung her up on the table. "Well, Miss Lindy, I'll go first," he said, rolling up his sleeve. He held out his arm where Lindy could watch, and let Maudie stick him with her four-pronged instrument.

She looked bemused, but gave him the same instructions she'd been giving the short people. "Now, if this turns red and puffy, you come back in a few days. Otherwise just keep it clean, all right?" she told him, her eyes sparkling in a way that reminded Jared of a dried apple doll with beads for facial features.

"Will do," he said, critically appraising her technique as she tested Lindy for TB. The child kept her thumb in her mouth the entire time, looking uncomfortable because Maudie was using the arm her thumb of choice was attached to and she had to make do with her spare. But she didn't whimper.

Jared set her down on the ground and stroked her pale hair, so soft it seemed to float under his hand. "Okay now, Belinda Marie?"

The thumb came out of her mouth with a pop, and she held it up and grinned. "Okay now."

"Then I'll get on with my work."

"Keep your arm clean," she told him solemnly. "Don't get no dirt in it, understand?"

"Understood. See you later, alligator."

Her giggle was sheer music as he strode down the hall.

He made it all the way to Randi's office and inside before he gave in to the urge to pound something. He chose one of the full metal filing cabinets, knowing it was too old and solid to give at his onslaught.

"All right, Galahad, which is it this time?" Randi sounded tired but unsurprised. "Want to clothe the entire preschool? Trade the minibus in for a Mercedes? Perhaps you noticed that one of the teachers, the one that looks the youngest, is almost as pregnant as Lindy's mama?"

Jared looked up to meet her weary but resolute gray eyes. "Aw, nuts. I missed that one altogether. No, it's just Lindy."

"Yeah. She's too thin and that jacket's had it, and best as I can tell, she's only got that one dress, two pairs of jeans and three tops."

He pounded the file cabinet again for good measure. "Lindy. Belinda. Do you know what that name means?"

"Never had the time for finding out."

"It's Spanish. It means 'beautiful.'" He swore fluently. "She's not beautiful. She could be, but she isn't. How can this be?"

"Oh, it's easy, Jared. Her father, when she had one, worked in the lead mines. When he got laid off two years ago, he looked real hard for another job for six months and, like most of the men, didn't find anything. There wasn't much to be found. Redbud Glassworks is the only company around here with a solid work force of more than twenty, and they're continually on the edge. So Lindy's daddy gave up looking and took up drinking. And then one night he took the Nicotine Express."

Jared's questioning expression didn't need words. Randi gave a wry grin and continued. "He went out for a pack of cigarettes and didn't come back. That was about seven months ago, right after Lindy's mom told him the good news about kid number three."

"So now she's raising two kids by herself, with another one on the way? God, Randi, no wonder you hate the male half of the human race."

"I don't hate much of anybody," Randi said. "I don't like the system that leads to kids like Lindy. She's going to be in deep trouble if she gets real sick. Or if her mama doesn't have a regular easy time of it when she delivers. But then, you've seen those kinds of facts of life."

"Not real often," Jared said, trying to ease the tightness constricting his throat. "Most of my patients could have bought and sold this clinic."

"Must be nice," Randi replied. "But I don't hate the man that left them all. He probably just couldn't handle it anymore. Lousy way to cope, but not all his fault. What about the system that doesn't have a job for him in the first place? I could hate that, but it's like hating rain. There's no purpose to it. I'd rather try to make sure Lindy's mom gets her prenatal vitamins and decent food for the three and a half of them, and wonder about where I can get some more clothes for Lindy and her brother."

"I could do that," Jared said.

"Yeah, you could. And Lindy's mom would tell you exactly where to put them, too," Randi said. She had that chin-out determined look again and Jared knew she was right. "No, if you want to go buy something that will make everybody happy, why don't you see how many sets of quilt batting you can fit in those motorcycle panniers."

"Quilt batting?" Jared had lost the train of thought somewhere.

"Yeah. We've still got months until our big raffle and festival, and the quilters could make four more doubles if they had the batting. That would give us about five hundred dollars more to run the center, resulting in funds that Lindy's mom *would* take. A Caring Place she'll take money from."

"Then I'll be back when I've got the batting," Jared said, striding out.

She called to him, and he turned. "Get some tinsel, too. The shiny silver kind. It really is time I started decorating inside for Christmas."

"Bah, humbug," he said, but he kept moving. Randi smiled, watching him go. Lindy had a champion. No, she told herself, it was more than that. The whole center had a champion. And he wasn't really a knight in shining ar-

mor either. More like a marshal riding in to make sure the
town was cleaned up.

"Who was that masked man?" she murmured to herself, listening to the roar of his cycle starting up. Jared
was coming around after all. The surge of love she felt for
him was warm and real and she got an idea. Perhaps the
marshal needed a little encouragement. Perhaps after a
very long session, school would finally be out.

Darkness still came early, not much later than six.
Jared was struggling with the bulky fluff of quilt batting, trying to shove another of his poorly tied bundles
onto the stack. Hell, how was he to know the things were
huge, but only weighed a few ounces? That each stupid
store would have only one or two, and that the lady behind the counter in the third place would break the news
to him that most folks that were particular about their
quilting used a double thickness. Hell again.

Jared tied the clothesline net he'd wrapped around the
unwieldly things a little closer. This time they would stay
put. They had to. It was getting dark and he was still
outside Redbud, and Randi was probably ticked at him.
She'd be sure by now that he'd headed for higher ground,
or was off bending his elbow somewhere. Of course she
had good reason for those beliefs, but it still rankled.

He got back on the motorcycle and started it again. It
roared to life and he headed on down the highway, careful of the curves. Finally he pulled up into the dark gravel
parking lot of the center. He looked around. No cars, no
minibus, nothing but Randi's battered old green heap.

No classes tonight? That would be a rarity. Maybe he'd
miscounted and Randi had her own class at the junior
college instead, that biology number she was always
studying for. He eased the clothesline ropes off one side

of the bike and started loading his arms with the batting.

It was ungainly to carry four of them at once. The slick plastic bags kept slithering away from him so that he lurched up the stairs. "All right, this better be unlocked," he muttered. Naturally, the door held fast.

Dropping the batting, he took off his helmet and dropped it on top of the puffy pile of wadding. Then he eased the key and chain off his neck. What a time for Randi to get security-conscious.

He kicked the whole pile inside the door. "Randi? I'm home," he called. While the phrase still rang off the hallway it stunned him. *Home?* How long had it been since he'd called anyplace that? Home.

Well, he was, he told himself, when no one else answered. The odd tan walls of his grade school room were home. The scarred walnut furniture was comfortable. In fact, the whole building usually had a welcoming air to it, as long as he didn't have to sleep in one of those cots.

He picked up the pile on the floor and went toward the room where the quilters usually worked. That, at least, was unlocked. He spilled the pile of batting onto the floor. "Randi?" he called.

Out in the hall there was still no answer. Jared noticed that the door to his room was open and there was light cascading from the doorway in a blinking glow.

He walked down the hall and stopped at the door. Pushing it open a little more, he stood still, not even breathing too hard for fear of disturbing the scene he saw inside.

It was Christmas in his room. There was no other phrase for the picture that met him. Randi sat in the battered rocker that normally was pushed back into a corner. Her head lolled back against the high back of the rocker and pale brown hair poured, unfettered, around her shoulders and down almost to her full breasts. Her pink lips were parted slightly as she breathed softly in sleep. She'd set up this whole wonderful scene for him and then fallen asleep waiting for him to come home.

And here he'd been angry because she hadn't opened the door.

Jared walked across the room as quietly as he could. He stood before the rocker, looking at the long-fingered, delicate hands in her lap over a pile of construction paper she'd been making into a lopsided red-and-green chain.

He expected it was intended to go on the kind of pathetic little artificial tree in the corner. There was a star on top, and a strand of twinkling white lights. One paper chain was already on the top half of the tree. So she was decorating for Christmas, and starting with his room first.

Where had she found the cowgirl's dream that she was clothed in? The camisole looked like a copy of old-fashioned ones tucked and ribboned forever. The shawl draped over it was black, and in a flash he knew that Christmas was in his room and Miranda had meant herself to be the present under this awful little tree.

Jared knelt, wondering how to wake her gently. He was cold from being outside on the bike. One touch of any of his flesh, even his lips, would startle her so badly, the chair would go over backward. But he had to wake her and quickly or go crazy looking at her. He'd have to settle for words.

"Miranda," he murmured softly. "I'm home. Wake up now, you hear?"

She came to slowly, as he thought Lindy might, a hand palm-out across her face and tangling in her hair. "I'm awake. Sort of. Ooh, is my neck ever stiff."

"Good thing that's all," Jared said. "I'd touch you, but I think I'm frozen. You are simply wonderful, Miranda."

She sat up now, putting her feet on the floor. Her growing awareness of what he saw started a flush that began at the top of her camisole and traveled higher. The portion of the flush that covered the tops of those soft, tempting globes made Jared ache all over. He wanted to bury himself there for good, but he knew he couldn't. One touch of his beard-roughened cold face and Miranda would be hanging from the overhead light fixtures.

"I'm a fool," she said to the silence that enveloped them both. "I don't know what I was doing, locking things up and getting rigged up this way."

"I do," he said quietly. "Or at least I think I do. But why now, Miranda?"

Her gray eyes filled with clouds. "I don't know. The time seemed right. You can't fix the whole world, Jared, but you sure want to try. You remind me of those old-time marshals, out to clean up the town. And I just decided the marshal needed a day off."

"Along with the schoolmarm?" He could feel his own smile warming his face.

"I guess so. But it's too much, isn't it?"

"It's not nearly enough," he said, finally taking her hands and drawing her to her feet. He willed her to ignore the spill of paper chain on the floor, and she did, looking at him instead. "I'm going to want so much more."

"Then take it, Jared. It's here for the taking."

He didn't expect her to be so hungry. Almost instantly her hands had buried themselves in his hair, and Randi stood on tiptoe while he sampled her lips, then went deeper, into much more than a taste.

Jared stifled the groan that was building inside himself. He picked her up, even though he was afraid of chilling her to the bone. Moving quickly, he deposited her on top of the quilt on his bed.

Everything went too slowly, from removing his cold, stiff leather jacket and boots, to trying to get rid of the turtleneck underneath. Finally he stood in nothing but black jeans that felt tighter by the second. Randi moved to unbutton her camisole, but his hand grabbed her wrist quickly. "No. Let me."

He eased the first few tiny buttons out of their restraining cloth. It seemed to take forever, reminding him of the skills he'd lost that Miranda would never get to see. The movement freed her breasts a little from their white cotton embrace, and Jared could resist no longer. "If I'm as cold as I think I am, push me away," he said. Then he nuzzled the warm flesh, flower fragrant and welcoming.

It wasn't just the building that made him feel at home, Jared realized. It was Randi. He could sense that she was still just as wary, still just as afraid, but still she was giving him the gift that she gave to no one else. All of herself.

"Let's go somewhere else," he said softly. "Somewhere that's maybe neutral ground for both of us. Close your eyes, Miranda."

She looked mystified, but she complied. He scooped her up again, blanket and all, knowing exactly where he was headed. There was a spot in one of the education rooms that looked little used and comfortable, and he intended to use it.

He kept carrying her, feet tucked up into her voluminous skirts and face hidden in his shoulder in such a way he nearly went mad from wanting her. He kicked open doors, flicked light switches with his elbows, until he set her down gently on some gym mats that were apparently stacked for use in natural childbirth exercises if the posters on the wall before he painted were any indication.

He was prepared for many things. What Jared wasn't prepared for was Randi looking around herself once and drawing into a horrified ball to burst into tears.

"Aw, hell. What did I do?" He was down beside her in a moment, holding her while she sobbed out her misery.

"You couldn't have known. Had no way of knowing. Oh, Jared, I can't be in here. Not for this." She bounded up and was gone in an instant. Jared grabbed the blanket and followed the floating white skirts down the dark hallways.

Finally she was nestled on her couch and he was wrapped around her. "Tell me now, everything. I have to know, Miranda."

"I don't ever go in there," she said. "It probably has cobwebs."

"Not anymore. I've been cleaning as I stowed presents there," he said. "But it looks like all the other rooms."

"It is, I guess. But it's the old fourth grade room."

"Did you have a bad time there as a kid?" Jared asked, still mystified.

"No. It's just that *she* belongs in there. Becki. My daughter. She'd be ten this year, in fourth grade. I just can't stand to go in there and be reminded of it."

"You have a daughter?"

"Had. She never drew breath," Randi said dully. While Jared pulled her tighter against his chest, facing outward so she didn't have to look at him, she told him the whole long story.

The yearnings of a young girl to be touched, loved, held. Of the boy who was all too willing to oblige her, and more. And then the realization that followed.

"It took me months to figure it out. I mean, I was as green as LoveAnne. I finally got the nerve to tell my parents."

"Alone? Didn't he go with you?" Jared could feel his jaw tensing.

"No. It's just as well. They threw me out of the house. I know it sounds melodramatic, but they did. My dad had always had a temper, and he told me to get and stay gone. My mom didn't argue."

Jared tried not to let his muscles freeze up. With Randi facing away from him, she couldn't see the anger in his face, and he wanted to keep her talking. Somehow he had to hear all of this, even the parts he could guess.

"Did he marry you?"

"He did. Quickly and with little fuss. We lived in this awful apartment over his grandma's garage. I worked at fast-food places, until I got too big for the uniform to fit." He could feel her shudder and drew her even closer. She seemed to relax a little.

"Finally I got so big, and I was so scared. The baby was moving all the time. It felt like a tidal wave in my belly. And then one day she stopped moving. I didn't know anything about having a baby. So I came to see Maudie. I'd saved up twenty-five dollars because I knew it was the cost of an office visit. I wanted to know if everything was okay and if I could have the baby in her office."

"What did she say?"

"She didn't have any words. By then my folks had moved away, so she couldn't skin them. And Billy just stood there looking like a scared rabbit. She took me back home with her and tried to break things to me gently. The labor started and ended that night. Billy was gone by morning."

Her breath left her in a long, shuddering sigh that rocked Jared to the core. "She was beautiful. Perfectly formed. Maudie couldn't tell me what went wrong. She's buried up in the old town cemetery."

Jared laid his head against her neck into the soft fragrant wealth of her hair. "God, Randi, I am so sorry."

She turned to face him. "So am I, Jared, but it doesn't change a thing."

He took her face between his hands, trying to be as gentle as possible. "But everything else changes things, doesn't it? All this work, all this worry. You're just trying to make sure LoveAnne and all her friends don't go through what you did."

"Yes. You understand. Does that mean you're going to help me?" It was little more than a whisper. Her eyes were misty, but no longer filled. In them Jared could see pain, but he could also see need and desire.

"Of course. Any way I can," he said, meaning every word of it. When her hands came up to bury themselves in his hair, it was no surprise.

She must feel the same hunger that he did, a hunger to erase pain and in its place put pleasure and healing. Her touch was igniting him, making him even wilder than he had felt before. He thought about nipping the rest of those buttons off clear down to her waist.

He knew they shouldn't be doing this, not now, but it was too late. Randi kept asking with her hands and her mouth and her body and Jared could only answer her need. His excitement was making his blood pound in his head, a steady thump that drowned out all other sound.

As he plundered the sweetness of her flesh with his mouth, the pounding got louder and more regular. Suddenly Randi was pushing him away and one look in her almost frantic gray eyes told him that the pounding wasn't his heart. It was someone beating on the front door.

Sitting still on her bed, he could hear the high, thin voices over the panic. "Get out of there, please, Miss Randi. The building's on fire," he heard.

Randi slipped off the bed and stood up. "You think they're right?"

Jared went out to the hall. From the back of the building he could see odd, hazy blackness. "They're right. Let's make a run for it, out the front." He threw the blanket over Randi and looked around the room for her shoes. They weren't anywhere to be found.

There was no time to look for more clothes, for everything he'd shed in his own room. "C'mon, Miranda, we've got to go."

She wasn't heading in the right direction. "But my records. And the quilts, all of them, they're hanging on racks back there, and all the Christmas presents—"

Jared actually growled as he picked her up bodily. She made a solid, struggling bundle, but he didn't yield. "We're going outside to wait for the fire department. Now."

"They're volunteers and they'll take forever," Randi said, on the verge of a sob.

"I've seen what fire does to people. It isn't pretty. We'll try to figure out what's going on, but we'll do it outside, Miranda. I am not about to stay in a burning building and neither are you." He put her down and shoved her none too gently toward the front door. She kept protesting but she went. Jared followed her.

Outside in the twilight they could see thick black smoke pouring out the windows of the basement at the foundation level. When they rounded the corner of the building, Loralee and LoveAnne lurched at them, sobbing in relief.

"You got out," LoveAnne shrieked. "I was so afraid you were going to burn up in there."

"I don't think there's anything burning upstairs. We would have noticed that," Jared said. "So far it's in the basement. Did somebody call the fire department?"

"On their way," a deep voice rumbled from nearby.

Carl. Jared looked at the bear of a man, standing in the gravel lot in front of the building. "Now what?"

"Now we wait and hope they come in time," Carl said, settling back against his cruiser to do just that. "A little bit of prayer wouldn't hurt if you're a praying man."

Jared wasn't. And watching the thick smoke continue to curl out of the windows, he suspected he wasn't a dreaming man anymore, either. His brand-new dreams of staying here, of being with Randi long enough to build some kind of life, were going up in smoke along with hers.

He held her while she raged and sobbed. The volunteers showed up in what felt like an eternity but was probably closer to ten minutes. A quick foray into the basement brought better results than Jared thought possible.

A tall young man came out, wiping soot off his face where his protective gear hadn't covered. "Furnace. Died of old age, I think," he said succinctly. "It's mostly smoke."

"So the whole building isn't going to go up?" Jared asked, beginning to be aware that he had half a blanket and a pair of pants and little else between himself and the night air.

"Not likely," the fireman said. "It isn't going to be livable for days. Too much smoke and soot. And it's probably going to damage the electrical system where the wires run down there. But no, the whole building isn't going to burn down."

Randi gave a whoop of hysteria and relief. "Can we go in?"

Jared gripped her shoulders even harder. "Don't you dare. You go over to Maudie's, or to one of the girls'. Don't even think about going back in that building."

"But my records. And presents, and the quilts—"

"Will still be there in the morning when it gets light, Miranda," Jared said sternly. "I'll make sure everything is okay, and it's all locked up. This is just too painful for you to watch."

Randi didn't argue with him. When she'd thought everything she owned, and everything she'd worked for, was going up in flames, she had been so stunned, she couldn't speak. Now that she knew she was going to have more work tomorrow than she knew what to do with, she felt cold and exhausted.

Jared settled all of the blanket around her shoulders. "Go on, now." He looked over her head as he squeezed her once, and Randi could tell that he and Carl were exchanging wordless male communication. She stopped even thinking of argument and let Loralee lead her over to the police cruiser.

In a few moments Carl came and drove her to Maudie's, where the doctor insisted she get a warm bath and go straight to bed. It was only by sheer force of will she fought off being given a sedative.

In the morning the light came too soon. Randi stumbled out of the strange bed and went to the window. From Maudie's upstairs, where the guest room was, she could see most of A Caring Place. At first her heart leapt to see the building, whole and looking relatively untouched. Then she noticed something that made her emotions plummet as she gripped the windowsill. Jared's motorcycle was gone. And so, she knew just by looking, was Jared.

She went downstairs to verify her suspicions. Maudie was dressed and making coffee in her antiquated kitchen. "He dropped off the keys to the building ten minutes after my kitchen light went on this morning," she told Randi. "I'm sorry, child, but he's gone."

The shock was bottomless. Just last night he'd told her, *promised* her he'd stay and help. Instead, there was a giant void where Jared should be. And thanks to the fire, she'd have too much to think about today, or for many days, to grieve the way she wanted to.

"Damn," she said succinctly. Maudie nodded. Randi looked out the kitchen window. "You think there's anything salvageable of all the gifts over there?"

"We'll find out," Maudie said. "But first you're eating breakfast."

Randi knew better than to argue, even though the thought of eating did nothing for her. "Yes, ma'am. Then we'll get to work."

"That we will," Maudie agreed. The percolator began muttering on the stove. The solemn chug of it echoed a phrase in Randi's heart. *Gone... gone... gone.*

Chapter Seven

A Caring Place stank of damp and soot and smoke. Randi stood in the hallway almost paralyzed by the thought of everything she had to do. She'd wandered around for an hour, surveying the damage. Now her feet were damp from the puddles in the basement and her hair smelled like smoke and her eyes stung from the acrid stench in the building.

At least the weather had changed. They'd gotten one of those strange warm spells that sometimes came in early December, and the place was full of water puddles instead of ice. That was a blessing, she told herself. It would make what she had to do next easier.

She rolled up the sleeves on her old flannel shirt and tied her hair back more firmly. Then she opened every window in every room. She shuddered a little when she went in the fourth grade room, but she opened all the windows in there, too. Jared had been right to be puzzled by her avoidance of the room. It was time for fresh air all over.

Once the windows were open, Randi went back to the room where her precious quilts were all hanging. She inspected the plastic bags that sheathed them on their hangers and wrinkled her nose. None were smudged but they all smelled awful. And the line to the dryer was part of the electrical system that wasn't working.

She thought about the old playground equipment rusting in the yard and wondered how many clotheslines she could string from it once she started washing quilts. "It better be plenty," she muttered.

It wouldn't be enough, she knew. Nothing would be enough to get the building back into shape quickly, especially not alone. The place echoed under her feet in a way it never had before.

This wasn't fair! Up until a few weeks ago she had liked being alone, even reveled in it. But now the building seemed like a cave without Jared in it. Around every corner she longed for a tall, dark presence with strong arms to gather her in and tell her this would all go away if she worked hard enough. She wanted the masculine smell of him, not ashes and smoke, to permeate things. Most of all she wanted to hear his laugh, which had been all too infrequent when he was around.

"Oh, stop wallowing in self-pity," Randi said out loud. It wasn't going to do any good. Jared was still just as gone. She wasn't sure which she was angrier about, his coming into her well-ordered life and messing it up, or his leaving just when she got used to his unnerving presence.

Whichever, she couldn't afford to sit around and feel angry right now, Randi told herself. Grabbing an armload of quilts, she headed for the washer. Once she got them taken care of, it would be time to find a bucket. Every wall and floor was going to have to be scrubbed before the smell of smoke and taint of soot was gone from the building.

By noon the man from the telephone company, who regarded her with the caution usually reserved for escaped lunatics, was wiring up a new phone line. And by two in the afternoon Randi had gotten down off her ladder to answer the silly thing three times. It was worth it, though, because each call was a client of A Caring Place who would be coming tomorrow to help her scrub walls and remove soot.

Just about the time it got too dark to really do any decent work in the half of the building without lights, the phone rang again. At first Randi considered just letting it ring, but whoever was on the other end was determined.

"I drove over to Park Hills once my office hours were over and got a bucket of chicken and all the trimmings. It's on the table and you better be here in ten minutes," Maudie commanded. Randi didn't argue. She didn't have time before the gruff doctor hung up.

Randi dumped her scrub water down the drain and went around closing windows. It had grown cold in the building and she noticed that she was shivering. She did a mental inventory. There was still a large empty place where Jared had been in her consciousness. But there were no tears. She was just too tired for tears. "Maybe tomorrow," she told herself as she shut the last window. Perhaps by then she'd have the time and energy for grief.

When she fell asleep over her second piece of chicken, Maudie marched her up to the old claw-footed tub upstairs and talked to her through the door so she wouldn't doze off again while she washed off the soot and grime.

Then she made sure Randi had a clean nightie and pointed her toward the guest room, where she spent what felt like ten minutes but was more like eleven hours before her shrieking muscles woke her to dim sunlight through clouds.

She pulled on more work clothes, braided her hair this time and pinned it tightly to the back of her head, gulped down a bowl of cereal and a cup of Maudie's coffee, her only culinary achievement, and went back to A Caring Place.

It was the pile of batting in the quilt room that finally reduced her to tears. Yesterday she'd ignored whatever was piled in one corner, figuring it wasn't as important as salvaging quilts and getting the office back in order. Today she went to investigate.

Sodden and smoky, still each in their plastic bags, were four quilt battings. "Oh, Jared, you really did it," she said with a sigh, and then her knees gave way and she sank down on the pile of ruined batting and finally wept.

The tears on her face were for so many things. For her dreams for Becki, ruined now a second time with the fire at A Caring Place. For letting herself get involved again with another beautiful male who in the end didn't stick around. For believing, even for a little while, that her life was going to be what she wanted it to be just because some man said so.

It was the banging on the front door that finally roused her. She used the back of one sooty hand to wipe the tears off her face and rose. "Coming," she called in irritation, feeling hoarse and scratchy from her crying jag. "Don't knock the door down. It's probably the best part of the building."

She flung it open to reveal two men in green uniforms, the older of the pair holding a clipboard. "We're here to install the new furnace and air," he said.

"Must be some mistake," Randi said. "I haven't ordered one yet. I mean, we need it, but—"

"Well, somebody thought you needed it enough to pay for it in full, lady," the man, who reminded Randi of a banty rooster, said, waving his clipboard. "How about you unlock the back someplace so we can get to work?"

Randi took the clipboard and looked at it, hard. The address was right and all the paperwork was stamped "Paid in full" already. And nobody had forged her name on the authorization signatures, either.

In fact, the scrawled signature seemed to read *Jared E. Tarkett, IV.* Jared? The tears blurred the papers in front of her again as Randi considered whether to howl or scream or let loose a rebel yell. It was some parting gift, anyway, and as bad as she needed it, Randi wasn't about to let pride get in her way of accepting it. It fell a little short of a miracle, and she would rather have had Jared, but if this salved his conscience as the back of that bike disappeared, well, so be it.

She looked up at the man holding out his hand for his clipboard. "I guess you're right. I'll meet you around back. The steps are steep and they're a little damp," she warned them.

"I imagine we've seen worse," the man said. "Just open those doors and we'll get to work."

They did, too. The noise was so fearsome at times, Randi thought the first floor would fall into the basement. The two of them lugged mangled parts of the old system up, and then sweated and swore the new system down while Randi kept scrubbing walls and hanging more quilts as they came out of the washer.

By eleven an electrician joined them, with another Tarkett-signed work order. Randi decided that if anybody else showed up, she was going to run them off the property. Even guilt had its limits. But no one else came, except Crystal, with Lindy and Curtis. She might have looked bigger than ever in the belly, and skinnier everywhere else, but she had a will to work. The children ran shrieking through the halls while the women scrubbed.

At one they broke for peanut butter and jelly sandwiches, a package of store-bought cookies and the last three apples in the refrigerator, cut up and shared around. Then the women put the children down on cots in the shelter room for naps, threatening dire consequences if anybody so much as moved an eyelash, and went back to scrubbing walls.

They were done with the front hall and moving down toward Jared's bedroom on that side of the building when Lindy's mom finally asked the question that Randi had been waiting for. "That Jared that was here helping you," she said, quirking one eyebrow. "He take off?"

"Right after the fire," Randi admitted, trying not to let her heartache show.

The other woman's slow, sad smile showed years of sympathy. Then her eyes brightened a little, getting slightly cynical. "That's a shame. He had a nice smile. In fact, he was nice looking all over, wasn't he? Sorry, Randi, I know he was yours, but I'm not blind," she said.

Randi was past caring. "He wasn't ever mine, Crystal." And that, she decided, was what hurt the most. In front of her, the wall grew slowly cleaner as the two of them worked in silence.

* * *

The furnace crew had to come back a second day to finish the new ductwork and test the system, which they pronounced functional by two o'clock the second day. By evening that day, the electrician, who had brought a helper the second day, pronounced his work done, as well. There was still one hallway that was sooty and smelled more of smoke than the rest of the building, and most of the gifts Jared had so carefully wrapped still sat in a ruined, sodden heap in the shelter room, but Randi decided to tempt fate and sleep at A Caring Place.

Awake, she was already resigned to the fact that Jared was gone, but three times during the night she started awake, sure she'd heard the thrum of a big motorcycle kicking up gravel as it skidded to a stop out front. By the third time she didn't even bother to get up off the narrow couch. It was all an evil dream. Jared was probably halfway to Alaska by now.

In the morning she got up and showered, marveling in the hot water that felt so good on her tired skin. The kitchen yielded nothing but cereal and milk and she made a mental note that sometime today she was going to have to get groceries if she had the energy.

Even with Christmas coming, her help gone, and a building to clean, the paperwork wasn't going to wait. Miraculously, although the office smelled smoky, it hadn't been water damaged. By ten Randi was riffling through various piles of papers while she scribbled furiously at a list and talked to someone from the state department of social services in Jefferson City.

When Carl pulled up and unloaded four huge pizza boxes out of the trunk of his battered cruiser, she looked at him through the window in puzzlement, but didn't dare interrupt the official she was talking to. Carl calmly went up the porch, pushed the front door open and took the pizzas somewhere inside.

When Sal pulled up behind him in a battered pickup, wrestled a pony of beer into the building and came back for a load of tools, Randi's puzzlement turned to sheer disbelief. She finally had to hang up when Ted Kimball's assistant and LoveAnne wrestled a huge floor polisher out of a van and hauled it up the steps.

"Just what is going on here?" she said in loud exasperation from the doorway. There were people all over her building going their separate ways.

"Work crew," Sal said succinctly. "Rest of them should be here in about half an hour. Scrub down the rest of the walls, clean the floors and set up the planning center in one corner of the gym."

"Planning center?" Randi asked numbly.

"For the fund-raiser," Sal said as if everyone knew. He looked around Randi's shoulder and raised his voice. "Hey, Carl, is Ben sure there isn't any problem with our setting up the bleachers that Friday afternoon? There's no pep rally or anything?"

Carl's roar came back. "Nothing on the calendar, according to Ben. I already told Jared the police explorer scouts would do the setting up. Heck, they want to be roadies."

Randi leaned against the door frame, her head spinning in confusion. "Somebody is going to tell me what is going on here. Now!"

"Well, it better be me, then," a deep voice came from behind her. "Because if I don't, you'll probably slap me silly."

Jared. Her spine was tingling even before she turned around to face him. He looked wonderful standing there in his familiar black gear, dark hair windblown. There were little lines around his eyes that she hadn't noticed before. They didn't half pay for what she'd been through the past two days. "Even if you do tell me what's going on, I might still slap you silly," she admitted. "Where the hell have you been?"

"Organizing," he said, eyes glittering as stubbornly as she was sure her own did.

"Hiding."

"Regrouping," he countered.

"Throwing money at a problem," she shot back.

"It needed money thrown this time, Miranda," he said. "Tell me it didn't."

She couldn't hold out any longer. "But, Jared, I needed you more," she told him. And then he was there, wrapping her in his embrace that smelled like leather and wind.

"Aw, babe, I'm sorry," he murmured, burying his face in her hair. She clung to his solid chest and hung on. Against all her beliefs, Jared was back. And what would she do with him now?

It was several hours before she really made sense out of everything that he'd done in two days. Randi marveled at the change in him. This Jared was wire-taut on his feet, bouncing with energy. He directed work crews from the twenty or so people that streamed into A Caring Place to clean and polish floors, replace battered window shades and give the basement a thorough going over.

Most of the Junior Service League was in the shelter room, taking apart presents and salvaging what they could. They'd brought a mountain of boxes and wrapping paper with them, and Randi suspected there were a few more dolls, toys and games that had made their way into the building with the teenagers, as well.

Jared supervised the setting up of tables and chairs in the corner of the gym where he, Carl and Sal palavered with several folks from the high school by midafternoon. It was when Randi got wind of what they were planning that she was the most stunned.

She sat in a chair, drinking the last cup of the third pot of coffee she'd made since noon. "Now let me get this straight, Jared. You know Stevie Joe Nash...."

"One of the few folks in Denton I'd still speak to on a bet," he said, cobalt eyes still sparkling.

"And you just got on the phone to him and asked him to do a benefit concert...."

"Well, you don't just get on the phone with Stevie," Jared said. "It takes more wrangling than a full-fledged audience with the pope. But finally I got hold of him, patched through on the car phone to his pickup and he said yeah, he expected he could be here in three weeks to do a show."

"And give the proceeds to A Caring Place?"

"And Redbud," Carl reminded her. "And a cut to the district high school for letting us use their gym."

"Why?"

Jared turned to face her fully and she was taken in again by the power in those blue eyes. "Why what? Why did Stevie Joe agree? Because he owed me one and he said it sounded like a hoot, anyway. He came up that way, playing high school gyms."

"No, more like why are *you* doing this?" And why did you come back at all? her unspoken question asked him in her eyes.

"I told you I'd help," Jared said simply, spreading his hands out on the bare wood table. "I figured the best I could do with my time was to bring in some support. In the long run it meant more than just sticking around to scrub walls, didn't it?" he asked, answering both of her questions at once in his own odd way.

"I guess so. But we're still scrubbing walls. And all of those calls could have been made from here."

"I couldn't do everything from here," Jared argued. "The heating contractor was in Park Hills, as was the automatic teller from which I got the cash to pay him."

"Whole trip would have taken an hour," Randi grumbled, picking up the coffeepot and heading toward the kitchen. Let them continue their planning meeting. Jared wasn't about to argue with her in public anyway, not the way she wanted him to. So she busied herself cleaning up empty pizza boxes, clearing away paper cups and going out into the hall to watch the volunteers finish the last of the walls outside the food pantry.

LoveAnne was wrapping the cord around the huge floor polisher so it could be wrestled back into the van. Her eyes shone in a way that was pure enchantment. "Hey, Miss Randi. Is what I heard true? Is Stevie Joe Nash really coming to play at the high school?"

"It appears that way," Randi told her, then watched as the girl did one of those little dances usually reserved for football players at the goal line.

"Yes, yes, yes," LoveAnne said. "I have to get tickets. Front-row seats."

"We'll try," Randi said. "Maybe we can even get Jared to introduce you sometime while he's here."

LoveAnne stopped dancing and stood stock-still. "Omigosh. What would I wear?" In thirty seconds she was out of the building. Randi could only lean against the wall and laugh at the strange turn her life had taken all in one afternoon.

The work crews broke up and left by the front door. Randi in her office could hear them telling each other goodbye. Then the meeting in the gym seemed to break up. She could hear Carl's heavy measured tread, and Jared helping Sal out with his mostly empty keg.

In a few minutes the door opened again, letting in the sounds of vehicles leaving the gravel lot; then it closed, and Randi heard the lock being turned. Then Jared strode into her office and stood in front of the desk. Still she didn't look up from the client files spread out in front of her.

"Well, Jared Eden Tarkett," she finally said, still studying the paperwork. "What in creation do I do with you now?"

"Damned if I know, Miranda," he said, drawing out every syllable in a voice that sounded more like Texas than anything she'd heard out of him yet. "You tell me."

She looked up at him then, wishing that looking into his face didn't give her a shock of recognition each time she did it. Just once she'd like to look at him and not have her heart leap. No, she decided, surveying his bright blue eyes, that might even be worse. At least this way she knew her body and mind were still capable of high levels of emotion and caring. Life had been so hard lately, she hadn't been sure, until Jared came back, that she could still care about anything anymore.

Looking at him, she knew she could care, passionately. He still stood in front of her desk, one hip cocked, the picture of arrogance, while he waited for her to answer him.

"I'd like to wring your neck, Jared," she said. "I figured you were gone for good."

"I would have said goodbye." His voice was quiet but intense.

"Would you? No one else ever has."

"I'm not anyone else, Miranda. I'm me."

She stood, pushing her paperwork away. "You can say that again. No one else could be so wonderful and so aggravating at the same time. Jared, what you've done for A Caring Place is so great. But now that you're back I want to wring your neck."

He looked more arrogant than ever. "What's the matter? Afraid I wasn't coming back?"

"As a matter of fact, I was. You just let the moment lead you. You didn't feel like staying around here, so you left. No word to anybody on when you'd be back, no word on what you were doing. Just left."

"I didn't just leave. I made sure the fire was put out first. And I locked up for you and gave Maudie the key."

"But, Jared, I expected to get the key from you in the morning. I needed you here. Leaving just isn't the answer every time."

"I know that, Randi."

She stood then. "Do you? It seems to be your stock response to everything, from what you've told me. You left Texas when you had one too many arguments with your father. You walked away from your whole career after your accident. And you've been leaving ever since."

"Not this time." His jaw was set in a hard line when Randi looked at him with some surprise. His tone was so much more forceful than she expected. "Not this time."

"Oh, yeah? Prove it. Tell me what was so different about getting on that bike this time and taking off."

"This time I wasn't going anywhere for good, or to get away from something," he said, striding across the office to the far wall, then turning back to her. There were high spots of color in his cheeks. "This time I was just getting a job done, one I knew nobody else could do as well as I could."

He stopped in front of her so quickly, she expected skid marks. "This time I was going *to* something, not away. You showed me, Miranda, that leaving isn't the answer. Sometimes it's harder to stay."

"It's always harder to stay," Randi said, finding edges of ice in her voice. "Can you promise that you will next time?"

His eyes held pain and determination. "You know I can't. Could you be satisfied with the fact that I didn't go yet?"

She hated his cool logic. It made her look into his handsome face again to look for signs of bitterness, or even the smug look she would have had herself if she knew she was that right. There weren't traces of either, and she sighed. "Not really. But that's the best I'm going to get. And I have to admit you did better wherever you were and I expect you had a better time in your nice, clean, quiet hotel room."

"Now that," he said, taking hold of her shoulders, "is where you are wrong."

Jared steered Randi away from her desk and gently eased her into the doorway of the office. "I did not have a better time in my hotel room. It was very clean but way too quiet, because I was alone."

Randi leaned against the door frame, too swamped in the nearness of him to do anything else. The cool metal of the frame was a relief. It brought some surcease to the pounding in her temples that had started when she looked up at Jared to see those flashing cobalt eyes engulf her.

He smelled of that mixture of leather and maleness that she'd come to associate with Jared and no one else. His hands kept kneading her shoulders as he continued to speak in a warm, slow rhythm that reminded Randi of hot molasses.

"It was too empty, Miranda. All I could think of was the woman I left behind, the one who had been waiting for me that night when I came back here. The one whose honey hair poured down her shoulders. The one who kissed me."

He leaned into her then and met her lips with his. At first the pressure was just a tentative sampling of the sweetness he brought from her, making her chest ache. Then, slowly, Randi found her fingers with a life of their own climbing Jared's back, twining in his thick hair, bringing his mouth to slant more deeply upon hers.

His tongue urged her lips apart and the sound he made when she welcomed him there was such a mixture of pleasure and pain that she could barely stay still. His hands were easing between her and the cold metal of the door frame now, removing her from that cool reality that stiffened her spine. She wanted to melt into Jared, using the heat of their kiss to puddle them both on the floor.

Then the phone that had sat on her desk silently for an hour rang. Randi's body was still firmly melded to Jared but her mind was treacherous. It had to answer that phone. He let her go, sensing the tension, and she kept herself from lunging for the telephone.

"She isn't here, is she?" he said above the noise. "That woman I left? She's gone away again, hasn't she?"

"I think so," Randi said, leaning back against the door frame again so her knees didn't collapse. "At least she's buried under so many other things right now, Jared. Give me time."

The phone stopped ringing before either of them tried to reach it. "I don't know how much time I have, Miranda," Jared said. He reached out to stroke her cheek with his fingertips, his expression almost wistful. Then he turned and strode down the corridor, leaving her to wonder where Jared's woman had gone and when she would be back. Because Randi knew that Jared's woman was the one she wanted to be, even though it meant a world of heartache.

Chapter Eight

Sometime during the night Randi woke up again, just as she had the night before, wide awake and listening. But this time it wasn't the real or imagined thrum of a motorcycle that woke her. It was the realization that they had less than three weeks to get ready for the biggest event Redbud had ever been part of, and it would benefit A Caring Place.

That didn't even mention the fact that all this would take place two days before Christmas. It was still dark outside and she made herself stay huddled in her nest of quilts. There would be time when it got light to grab one of her ever-present legal pads and start making lists and jotting notes. The new Jared who'd come back seemed very organized. Surely, together they could pull this thing off.

She thought back to their conversations of the day before. He hadn't ever professed undying love, but he had come back. He had reminded her, and everyone else, that he had promised to help her. Randi wondered how soon she could start easing him into help he was actually qualified and trained to provide, like taking over for Maudie so that she could finally take her desired, deserved retirement.

If nothing else, Maudie should get to spend Christmas with her sister in Hot Springs. Lord knows she always told them about it when she didn't get to go. Looking up toward the ceiling, Randi decided she couldn't rush this. Jared was back and he was enthusiastic, but he would have plenty to do until after the concert. Then she'd talk to him about being Dr. Tarkett again. He *had* promised to help. And to Randi that meant only one thing.

Somewhere in her reverie she dozed off again, and it was full light when she rolled out of her quilts and put her feet on the hard, cold floor. Padding to the window in her socks, she looked out to assess the day. There were bright blue skies and a brisk breeze fluttered the still-bare branches of the tree outside her window.

It was another fluttering that caught her eye. In the yard was that poor little artificial tree she'd put in Jared's room. It was on a huge stand and seemed to be totally covered with large lights and streamers of tinsel. In the dark it wouldn't be half bad, she suspected.

Jared had replaced her Christmas tree. That little gesture said more than anything else he'd done so far. She knew if she'd say anything he'd deny it, so she just smiled and hugged herself a little at the cold window. Christmas was coming, whether she was ready or not. Maybe, just maybe, this one would be different.

Jared was up and dressed, and pacing around the kitchen, grumbling, when Randi walked in. "We are going grocery shopping the moment you get ready," he said. "I had to raid the food pantry to find biscuit mix for breakfast."

"You cooked?"

"It's not brain surgery, Miranda. Even I can make drop biscuits."

"News to me. I never saw you make a sandwich before, Tarkett," she countered.

"Never had to. You always beat me to the kitchen." His smile was irritating this early in the morning. "And I have to admit that things that require a minimum of mixing and direction reading are about as far as I can go."

"Well, that's a relief," Randi said. "I was afraid I'd really had you pegged wrong."

His answering grin was wry. "No, most of the time you've got me pegged about right, lady. Are we totally out of butter?"

"Yep. The refrigerator was on the electrical circuit that died and I gave away everything I could that first day and moved the rest to Maudie's. We've got some grape jelly someplace."

"Beats dry biscuits," Jared said. "I did save the coffee making for you. Mine is awful."

"Too strong," Randi said, knowing just by knowing Jared. "And you probably never wait long enough for it to brew, impatient soul that you are."

He was in front of her then, hands buried in her hair, pulling her toward him. "You do know me too well. And I'm also too impatient to wait any longer for a good-morning kiss." He lowered his head and took the kiss, savoring her lips. "Be forewarned, I'll never get enough of this. I'll be good while there are clients around, but things are going to be different now, Miranda. I'm not going to hold back all the time."

"Then we better get plenty of groceries, because I'll have to keep you so busy, your tail is dragging by sunset every night," she teased him.

"We'll take the car. That much food won't fit on the cycle."

"No one ever said it would, Jared," she said, reaching up and tugging on his dark forelock. "Now help me make the list while we eat."

It was like that for two solid weeks. When Jared wasn't bantering with her, he was working every moment it was light. And somehow in between they always found time for a hug in the supply closet, a quick kiss in the hall when they were alone. But never for long. And somehow, by mutual unspoken agreement, about nine each night they went their separate ways. Randi had never told Jared she wanted to be left alone then, but by then her resolve was worn thin and she suspected his was, too.

It was a nightly battle for her to keep from edging down the worn tile to his room, where she could hear the radio playing softly. But it just wasn't the time to deepen her relationship with Jared, not with everything else going on. That would have to wait until after Stevie Joe Nash had come and gone.

The posters trumpeting his arrival were plastered all over the county. Radio stations gave them free airtime for commercials. And the Junior Service League volunteered to sell tickets once they were printed up, which didn't take long. There was always a flurry of girls around the office any moment school was out, ticking off lists, filling the battered cash box, offering to go to the bank.

LoveAnne was the chief offender. Randi threatened to monitor her next report card, because she couldn't be studying. "Aw, Miss Randi, I'm passing everything. At least straight B's without studying, you know that," she argued. "Besides, this is *Stevie Joe Nash.*" She said it with a reverence rarely reserved for mere mortals, and Randi quit arguing. It would be easier to argue with a wall.

So there was little time, at least in that second week, to be alone with Jared. The Junior Service League inadvertently saw to that.

During the weekend the enthusiasm mounted to a frenzy. Most of the concert tickets were sold by Sunday night and Randi shooed the last teenager out the door at eight, determined to have the building to herself with Jared in it for a little while. But while she was locking up he was zipping that leather jacket. "Need to go out and clear my head," he said. "Come with me?"

She hadn't ever considered it before, but tonight it sounded good. "You have a second helmet?"

"Have had for weeks," he said. "I've just been waiting for you to ask."

"Yeah, well you would have waited 'til doomsday, because normally I wouldn't get on a motorcycle for love nor money," she told him. "You must have caught me at the right moment."

He turned toward his room. "I hope so. Let me go get that helmet."

It was a new experience, zipping down the dark country highways with her hair flying out behind the helmet. Randi decided she liked it, as long as it was Jared's broad back and narrow hips she was clinging to in front of her. Resting her cheek on his jacket, she let the cold air rush by, watched the trees flash in quick succession.

When he drove all the way to Park Hills and pulled into a drive-in, she was a little surprised. "I've got this sudden craving for ice cream," he explained, grinning. "Join me?"

Randi laughed. "You just want to get me cold enough so I'll hang on to you like that again all the way home," she teased.

"You could drink hot coffee and you'd still hang on like that, I'd bet," he answered her.

"You're right. But I'll have a hot-fudge sundae just to make you happy."

Monday at midmorning the shiny silver tour bus pulled into the lot at A Caring Place and the circus began. Stevie Joe came down the steps and shook Jared's hand, slapping him on the back at the same time. "Hey, Jared," he said in a voice that was too loud for Randi, but friendly. "You look pretty good for a hermit."

"Now, who told you I'm a hermit?" Jared answered.

"Nobody. I just figured—you're out in the middle of nowhere, over a thousand miles from the last place I saw you. I mean, I'll bet there isn't even a decent hospital for fifty miles, so you can't tell me I'm still looking at Dr. Jared Tarkett."

Jared's face darkened. "You know that's over with, Stevie." Randi wanted to come and slip a protective arm around him, but she held back at the doorway, waiting for an introduction. Or perhaps now it was going to be a fight instead. But Jared surprised her by just shaking his head and breaking into a grin. "You'll see what I mean. This isn't the middle of nowhere. It's a great little place. By Friday you'll be ready to buy acreage yourself."

"That will happen when Bo grows antlers instead of sleeping in the back of the tour bus," Nash countered. "So start showing me around."

The tour started at the foot of the steps, where Jared introduced Randi to the country star. Up close she could see he was young, probably under twenty-five. Randi thought she ought to have known that, if she'd paid attention to the girls, but it was a little bit of a surprise to see his youthful face under the dark Stetson. His hair, when he swept the hat off to say hello, was pale, almost silvery blond, and his eyes an arresting green. Randi began to see why LoveAnne went all funny every time she talked about him.

The band members filed off the bus, followed by Bo, a mostly boxer brindle dog with an amiable manner at odds with his huge size. He seemed to take to Randi immediately, among much laughter. "Bo's not usually a lady's man, or dog, or whatever," Stevie explained while the dog made lovesick moans around Randi's hand scratching behind his ears.

"Oh, he's just a big baby," she said, enchanted by his goofy demeanor. That brought guffaws from several band members.

"Heck, I've seen him nearly take an arm off grown men," one of them said. "He's never acted like this to anybody else except Stevie Joe."

"He has good taste," Jared said, slipping an arm around her waist. Bo's head came up briskly and he sniffed judiciously before deciding Jared's arm could stay where it was.

"Do you have hotel reservations someplace close? Park Hills, I guess, if anywhere," Randi said.

"We got rooms for just about everybody," Nash said. "Bo and I stay in the tour bus by ourselves. We both like it that way better than hotel rooms."

"Yeah, that's just because of that one place where he ate the drapes. Stevie's too cheap to pay for another hotel room trashed by that old dog,'' a band member drawled.

"You're giving away all my secrets, Asa,'' Nash said. "How about we see the inside of this place and then head on over to the school?"

"You'll probably want to wait until after two for that,'' Randi warned. "Let the bus get off the lot first. Otherwise you'll cause a stampede of teenage girls."

Jared laughed. "Listen to the lady, Stevie. Even Bo couldn't hold back this crew."

"Fine,'' Nash said. "But I'll have to meet at least one of them before the concert. I've got a bit in the show where I bring a girl up on stage with me."

Randi and Jared looked at each other and spoke at the same time. "LoveAnne."

"That's really somebody's name? Aw, perfect,'' Stevie Joe said. "Now show me the building. Quickly, before Bo decides to lose his good behavior." Randi gave a lightning tour of the facility before offering to feed the whole band, dog and all, when Maudie came in for lunch.

She wondered what the older woman would have to say about the collection of turquoise, silver and denim on the other guests and the number of long-haired males. Knowing Maudie, it would be worth listening to, she told herself as she headed for the kitchen to make sure the pot of chili was big enough. It was the first time she'd ever cooked with a smitten dog following at her heels, muttering to himself in canine delight. Jared's expression as he walked by showed that he didn't know whether to laugh or cry. "I won't get a private moment with you again, not until that dog leaves town,'' he said.

"You invited him here, Tarkett,'' she reminded him.

"I invited the man. I didn't invite the dog. He just showed up to be a nuisance." In response Bo sidled a little closer to Randi and curled his lip while staring at Jared. Randi couldn't help but laugh as she patted his big head.

"You're just jealous," she told Jared.

"Correct as usual," Jared replied, heading for the bus to help unload. He pointed a finger at Bo. "Saturday morning. You'll be gone and I'll be the one getting the pats on the head."

"If that's what you want," Randi said.

He turned around, still smiling. "No, but that's all you're giving him. Not even you would kiss that monster on the lips."

"You're right," Randi said, wrinkling her nose. She looked down at the slobbering jowls below her. "Don't take it personally. I don't kiss anything with four feet."

"And precious little with two feet," Jared said as he went out the door. "But that part's just fine with me, as long as I'm on the short list."

Every morning that week when she woke up, Randi found her new constant companion waiting for her. They'd given Stevie a key to the building and he used it each morning to come in and get coffee going and let in the dog. Bo then lay in the doorway of Randi's room until she opened it and he padded in to kiss her hand and fawn at her feet.

"You're going to be so spoiled by Saturday," she told him as he gave her a big doggy grin. "What are you going to do when Stevie puts you back on that bus full of guys?"

"Moan and whine for about three days, I'll bet," Stevie said as the pair walked into the kitchen. "Morning, Randi."

"Morning." Bo left her side long enough to say hello and then came back when she was seated at the table with a mug of Stevie's coffee. The young man surprised her. Randi had expected some spoiled prima donna.

Instead, there was an open, friendly country boy who could have been one of the local high schoolers a few years back, except that this country boy was drop-dead handsome. It was also apparent at second look that his boots probably cost more than her entire wardrobe, and his faded jeans were custom tailored. But Stevie Joe himself never called attention to those things.

He'd spent the early part of the week wandering back and forth between the high school, for preliminary sound checks and layout, and A Caring Place, where he seemed intrigued by all the programs that his concert funds would help promote.

The food pantry got two cases of chili and three of powdered milk hand-delivered by band members after he'd gone through there. And he insisted that the brightest of the log cabin quilts be put in the bus and wrote a handsome check, more than twice what they would have gotten at auction, for the piece.

"Now I'll just have to figure out how to keep this miserable dog off it," he told Randi, scratching behind Bo's ears.

"Just tell him to stay off," she said. "It works for me."

"For whatever reason, he'd walk over coals for you." Stevie sipped some more of his coffee. "You seem to have that effect on man and beast. If anybody told me I'd ever see Jared Tarkett tethered to a town of less than three hundred people, I'd never have believed it."

Randi looked at him. "Had it been that bad, before?"

Stevie nodded. "I'd see the man I knew and there'd be nobody home. Next I heard he'd taken off on that bike and nobody could find him. His daddy had private investigators out looking for traces."

"Was he that interested in finding him? From what Jared said, I'd gathered they didn't get along."

"They didn't, not exactly," Stevie said. "But that man dearly loves his assets, and the Tarkett Clinic is the biggest one of those. To lose Jared's services probably hurt more than actually losing Jared."

"Did he ever find him?"

"Not to my knowledge," Stevie said. "I haven't seen the man for months myself. He quit calling and coming around last fall. Jared hasn't called home or anything from here?"

"Not that he's told me about," Randi said. "But, then, he doesn't tell me everything."

"Just mostly everything." Stevie Joe grinned. Bo heard the laughter in his voice and looked up, putting his head on Randi's knee so that he could follow the conversation better.

"Well, maybe so," Randi admitted. "Has he always been this much of a . . . private person?"

"To the death," Stevie said. "He's been here, what, maybe five or six weeks, and you know more about him than I found out in forever."

"Oh." The dog seemed to sense Randi's surprise because he nosed her palm, looking for attention. She stroked him absently while she thought. She felt disloyal pumping Stevie for information. But Jared didn't volunteer much and there was so much she wanted to know.

"Did he have any other real good friends in Denton?"

Stevie's green eyes glimmered. "Like lady friends? Nope. You've got no Texas competition." The wink he gave her made Randi giggle.

"How about me? Do I have Texas competition?"

Jared was lounging in the doorway and to anyone else he would have looked casual and friendly. But there was an edge to him that Randi saw immediately.

She was at his side in a flash. "What on earth would I do with two of you? One disagreeable Texan around here is plenty. But I might point out that Stevie Joe managed to pull his vehicle into the lot without knocking anything over."

Jared's mock growl of aggravation brought Bo to his feet. His tail swept the corner of the table, sending sugar packets, creamer and napkins flying. "So much for not knocking things over," Jared said as he helped clean up the mess. Only Randi saw the pat on the head he gave the dog, who seemed to grin like a conspirator.

The rest of Thursday was taken up with planning and plotting, and calming a pacing LoveAnne.

"Are you sure I shouldn't have my hair done like for the prom?" she asked Randi, twisting nervous fingers with pale pink tips.

"No, I'm positive." Randi stopped her motion, taking the girl by the shoulders. "Remember, Stevie Joe said he just wanted a normal-looking girl. Wear exactly what you would have worn to the concert anyway, no bunches of makeup, no tortured hair."

LoveAnne swallowed convulsively and nodded. Randi looked at her hard. "Are you sure you don't want to meet him beforehand? He said it would be okay."

"No. Not until after whatever this is," LoveAnne said. "Maybe I'll be less nervous then. At least I hope so. What if I pass out or throw up or something?"

"You'll do fine," Randi said. "Don't worry so much about it. Just do all the things we've talked about in class all these years. I mean, you've been on six job interviews and four college admissions meetings, sweetie. Surely this isn't more important."

The look she got in return told Randi how important this was. For LoveAnne this was the meeting of a lifetime. Randi patted her shoulder again. "Confidence. Poise. Grace under pressure." She gave the young woman a quick kiss. "Now go on home and call Loralee. She'll convince you more than I will."

"I guess so," LoveAnne told her, heading for the door. Randi watched her go, her slight shoulders not looking big enough to carry the weight she was obviously putting on herself.

"Whatever happens, it will be over tomorrow night," she told herself. "And then we can get back to normal around here."

She said that more than once during the busy day with what seemed like hundreds of people coming in and out of A Caring Place with last-minute plans. Stevie Joe was always in the middle of it. She and Jared never had a moment alone together, but Randi wondered if that wasn't just as well. He disappeared with Stevie around six to go out to dinner. Randi knew they'd gone to Jared's favorite café in Park Hills when Stevie came back raving about chicken-fried steak and cherry pie.

"You're right about this place," he said as they came in the door together. "You think there's any property around here for sale? I'm awful homesick for good country again after a couple years on the road."

Randi bounded up from her desk. "Mr. Nash, if you're serious, I could put you in touch with five or six people who'd be thrilled to sell you acreage. Some with houses already on it, some where you could build. Just say the word."

His shaggy blond head went back in a healthy laugh. "She always this enthusiastic?"

"Only when you are talking about her pet subject, which is anything that might benefit at least one citizen of this fair county," Jared said.

Stevie laughed again. "Would you be that enthusiastic about listening to us rehearse? I thought we could work out a little in the gym here just to get in form for tomorrow night."

"Sure," Randi said. She was anxious to see the young man perform after living around him for most of a week. "Bo coming in, too?"

"Wouldn't rehearse otherwise," Stevie said. "It's the only way I know when we're in top form. He wants to dance."

Randi didn't think that was possible until she saw it happen. But Stevie Joe and the band did have an infectious rhythm to their music. By the third number, Jared had pulled her to her feet and they were moving quite naturally together.

It was the first time in days she'd been in his arms, and Randi felt right at home there. With Jared she felt young as the music and feisty, as his muscled arms guided her around the floor.

His grin reminded her of a wolf again as the next number slowed and he pulled her closer. "Thought I was going to have to pay them to play a slow one," he murmured in her ear.

There was still the tang of wind in his hair from being out on the bike during the day, and she reached out to touch the faint crinkles around his eyes. "I'm glad they did. Play a slow one, I mean. I've missed you."

His lips brushed her forehead. "Um. Me, too. This is great. Wonder if we can convince them to do two in a row like this?"

"You may not want to," Randi warned him, seeing Bo over his shoulder. "We're about to have company."

The boxer nosed his way between their bodies, nearly bowling them over.

"Big mutt. Come on, go find your own partner." Jared growled, trying to push the dog from where he was determined to stay. Bo slid out from between the two of them and circled around Jared, putting his oversize front paws on Jared's back, almost to his shoulders.

"I think that's a hint," Randi said, giggling. "No, Bo. Go on now and lie down. I'll dance with you later."

He whined, but he went. "I don't believe it." Jared watched him turn around before settling into a corner.

"Well, you'd better believe it, because you get one more song, partner. Then I go keep my promise."

"To a *dog?*" His voice was unbelieving.

"To a dog. Or to anybody else, Jared. You know how important promises are to me."

"I've only begun to learn." He settled back into nuzzling her hair. "Lord, woman, I hope I never have to break one to you."

Randi suppressed an involuntary shiver. "That makes two of us." The band played on, segueing two slow songs together until Randi had to pull away just to catch her breath.

Bo trotted up hopefully. "He knows he's next," she told Jared. "Hey, Stevie, play a fast one. I've got to dance with Bo."

"He only knows the Texas Two-Step," Stevie hollered, launching into a rowdy number that kept the dog skipping around the room, tongue hanging out in pleasure, as Randi skipped with him and Jared watched them both in silence, shaking his head.

The next twenty-four hours passed in a blur for Randi. She marshaled people in and out of places, held Love-Anne's hand, saw plenty of Jared, but only moving at a fast clip. They were both always moving, it seemed. There was plenty of equipment to carry, last minute details to finesse.

She didn't really remember eating or drinking anything all day besides bites and sips of things grabbed while standing up. Her concert clothes, new jeans and a clean Western shirt, had been slid into hurriedly. She gave a little more care to her hair, catching up the cascade with an ornate bow, which Jared insisted had to include a sprig of mistletoe.

When he saw her, all dressed and ready, Jared approved. His eyes shone in the half dark of the hallway when they met briefly before the concert. "Wish us luck or something," he murmured, holding her close for too brief a moment. "I think we're going to sell out."

"Great," she said. "Now if the fire marshal doesn't come along to see how many folks you've got squeezed in the bleachers, we're okay."

"I know we're okay," Jared said with a grin. "I just sold the fire marshal the last five bleacher seats."

Carl and his two officers strode around the floor keeping order. The crowd was surprisingly well behaved.

Looking out, Randi could see LoveAnne and Loralee sitting in the front row. LoveAnne looked about as cheerful as someone facing the firing squad. Loralee didn't look much better.

Jared was standing next to one of the sound men, doing last-minute level adjustment. There was a spotlight beaming on him and Randi reveled in the silver glow that seemed to emanate from the fringe on his black jacket. Black and silver, that was Jared; dark and elusive and fast as moonlight to change. After tonight, would he be on the road again? The concert had been such a focus for all of them that Randi wasn't sure. And if he did stay, where would they go from here? Randi knew where her heart could easily lead her, but Jared's feelings were as hidden from her as ever.

She wished Maudie were here to hold her hand. Randi was beginning to regret talking her into going to Hot Springs. She'd enjoy all the commotion of the concert. Still, it was nice to think of her playing bingo with her sister.

The seats were all filled and Stevie Joe and the band were pacing backstage. Then suddenly the band went onstage, there was a lot of cheering and whistling and Stevie Joe winked at her once, jammed his hat on his head and strode out into the light.

The show was electrifying. Randi enjoyed each number more than the last until Stevie Joe, looking like he'd run a marathon, put down his guitar and picked up a mike. "I want to do a love song for you now," he said. "Anybody here in love?" He looked down into the audience, which had gotten very still. "This young lady here looks like a likely candidate."

He went down the steps to take LoveAnne's hand. She stood like a deer caught in headlights, moving only when he smiled at her. "Come on up here with me, darlin'," he said. "What's your name, sugar?"

"L-L-LoveAnne."

"Well, LoveAnne, are you in love?"

She nodded and Randi found tears springing into her own eyes. "Can you tell me with who?"

LoveAnne shook her head. "He doesn't know," she said, her voice hardly more than a whisper as she looked up at her idol.

"He doesn't know," Stevie echoed, his voice incredibly tender. Randi couldn't help but search for Jared's face. Did he know? Could he possibly?

"Well, how about I sing this anyway for him, okay?" Stevie said. They were standing up on the stage again now, facing each other in the spotlight. He never let go of the girl's hand as he began his love song.

It was slow and sweet and impossibly romantic. Through the entire song those green eyes were riveted on LoveAnne, who looked right back at him in a glazed way. Randi knew the girl was unaware that tears were rolling down her cheeks, making the moment even more bittersweet. But Randi's thoughts were elsewhere, on another man who had touched a woman's heart. In some ways, she felt just as lost and powerless as poor LoveAnne.

When the song ended there was a hush for a moment, and then a giant roar from the audience as Stevie Joe leaned over, kissed LoveAnne on the forehead and pointed her back to her seat.

"He's lucky, whoever he is," he said. "You going to tell him?"

She managed to smile a little. "I don't know," Randi heard her say. "This might be enough all by itself."

"I hope so," Stevie said into the mike. "Well, that was for LoveAnne's feller, whoever he is. And it was for all of y'all, too. There needs to be lots of love at Christmas-time. Love and miracles. Merry Christmas." As Love-Anne left the stage, the band picked up in a rowdy chorus, and Stevie played one fast number that brought the crowd to its feet as he left the stage.

Jared was there in the wings, and they were back slapping each other even before the lights dimmed. "You did it, partner," Jared crowed. "You're a Christmas miracle all by yourself. We've got a cool twenty-five grand, and that doesn't even count the quilt auction during intermission. We're in the black, Stevie. Thanks."

"My pleasure," he said. "I think tomorrow I'm going house hunting. These folks do appreciate a good song."

Suddenly Jared spotted Randi. "Hey, Miranda. Good job, huh?"

Randi could only smile. She was feeling such a tangle of emotions, she didn't know what to say. She simply accepted Jared's welcoming embrace.

After a moment, he pulled away. "Say, what's this? Have you been crying?"

Randi hastily wiped her eyes. "I'm just glad it all worked out so well."

Jared looked skeptical, but before he could question her further, they were interrupted by Loralee. She looked worried. "Crystal's here, Randi. I think we've got trouble."

One look told Randi she was right. Crystal's face was pinched and a pale shade that only emphasized her tightly set features. "Oh, no. Not tonight."

"Tonight," she said, still clutching the tiny hands of both children beside her. "And awful quick."

Chapter Nine

"How on earth did you get here?" Randi asked Crystal.

"I drove." The two words spoke volumes more about what a chore that had been. "It was the only place I could think of where I might get help with Maudie out of town."

Randi tried to gather her wits in the noise and confusion of the backstage area. She was going to have to break her promise to Jared. Folks were going to have to know, tonight, that he was a doctor.

Pulling a battered plastic and metal chair from a corner, she settled Crystal in it. "Sit here for a few minutes. I'll get some people I need to and then we'll go back to A Caring Place in my car."

Crystal nodded, her eyes almost as wide as Lindy's and Curtis's. Randi pushed through the crowd. Of all the nights for this to happen!

In front of the stage LoveAnne was still mobbed with friends. "Do not leave," Randi told her. "In fact, come backstage with me now." She turned to Ted. "I may need your daughter all night. Crystal's gone into labor and she's got those two little ones with her."

Ted smiled. "Say no more. I'll look for her home when she gets there and know she's in good hands."

Randi blinked, but she took an unprotesting Love-Anne and went back to the cavernous back of the stage area. For Ted not to argue over something like this was unusual. Maybe instead of a disaster, this was one of those miracles she'd been looking for.

While they worked their way back to Crystal, Randi filled LoveAnne in on the situation. "I don't have to watch, do I?" she asked.

"Just these two, sweetie. Nothing more than that, and you've done that before," Randi said reassuringly. She thought of herself, LoveAnne's age and having a baby. It didn't seem possible. No wonder she'd been bewildered and terrified.

Jared had taken Stevie aside and told him of the latest development. The news was spreading through the band like wildfire, only heightening their already elevated spirits. Jared stepped aside to consult with Randi when he saw her return. "We can't do anything here," he said. "How're we getting her back to the center?"

"I figured in my car. She drove over here, but she wasn't really in any condition to do that."

His brow furrowed even more. "I'd say not." He swore roundly. "Why in creation did you ever tell Maudie to go to Arkansas?"

"Because she said Crystal wasn't due until the middle of January, and besides, she hasn't had Christmas with her family since Carter was president," Randi fumed.

"Great. She gets Christmas in Hot Springs and we get to deliver a baby."

"We?" Randi squeaked.

"We. There's no way in hell I can do this alone, Miranda. Get her back there and get ready for a long night."

Randi gulped and nodded. Stevie touched her shoulder as she got ready to go. "You say this lady has two little kids with her."

"Yes. LoveAnne Kimball is going to look after them."

He seemed to be speculating. "Asa and me, we were going to stay around here for Christmas, anyway. The rest of the crew is all going into St. Louis and catching planes for home, but we neither of us have more family than Bo. So why don't we take the kids and Miss LoveAnne and keep them in the bus out of your way?"

"That would be above and beyond the call of duty," Randi said. "But if you want to..."

"Wouldn't have offered if I didn't," Stevie assured her. Randi brought him over to LoveAnne and the little group clustered around her. No real introductions were necessary. He and LoveAnne seemed to communicate without using any words, and the children accepted that this tall, shiny stranger was all right with their friend LoveAnne, so he'd be all right for them, too.

Crystal looked grateful until a contraction bent her over in the act of getting out of the chair. She sat back down until it passed; then she and Randi hurried out to the car to try to get settled before the next one overtook her.

There were lights on in several places at A Caring Place when they got there, and both the silver bus and the motorcycle were in the lot in moments. Randi parked hurriedly and went inside, helping Crystal up the stairs.

An hour later, Randi wasn't sure who looked paler, Jared or Crystal. They'd settled her as comfortably as possible on his bed because it was the largest in the place. It seemed odd, the smell of leather and Jared in the room, Christmas garland strung from corner to corner, and Crystal in the throes of hard labor.

"C'mon," Jared coached her. "We're going to make it through this. And remember, you give me plenty of warning if you feel any different."

"You'll...get as much warning...as I do," Crystal promised. Randi looked up at Jared, trying to forget the pressure Crystal was putting on her hand. She wasn't sure that she'd be able to use her fingers in any meaningful way for days the way they were being squeezed.

Jared looked as stressed as she felt. He hadn't looked this gaunt since the night he'd come here. Still, his energy level was high and he was encouraging the woman who needed him the most.

Randi was glad he hadn't complained about her telling Crystal his secret. She was relieved to have him there, even if he wasn't too sure about how he was doing. And Randi had to admit that she was probably as relieved as Crystal.

She knew that helping women have babies would be part of her life if she ever finally got to be a general practitioner in someplace this small. But she hadn't expected this first experience to bring back all her old ghosts.

Seeing Crystal pale and sweating, stomach rippling with contractions, brought back all the fear and anger of so long ago. There was no reason to believe that this would be anything but a healthy baby, but still Randi found herself on edge in ways she hadn't anticipated.

"You going to be okay if we go collect some more supplies?" Jared asked Crystal.

"Long as you don't leave the building or anything," Crystal said, trying to moisten her dry lips. "Stay within shouting distance and I'll be okay."

"Don't worry. Any chance you could try to sleep between these contractions?"

"Not enough time," Crystal answered.

"We'll be right back, then," Jared said, giving Randi a pointed look so that she would follow him.

She was reluctant to leave Crystal, but Jared seemed to need her more, alone, right now. She followed him into the kitchen, where he started handing her clean towels and a large basin.

"The other stuff will be in the cabinet Maudie uses to store her supplies in," Randi said. "You all right?"

"As good as I'm going to be," Jared said.

"You'll do all right," she told him.

"What I hope right now is that *you'll* do all right, because you're going to be doing more than I am, once this kid actually makes his or her appearance."

Randi felt a thrill of panic run through her.

"What do you mean?"

He flexed his right hand in front of her. "Really want me catching a newborn with this? If I can't sign my name properly, I'd hate to think I'm going to try the intricacies of birth. But I know what things should look like, and I can talk you through anything I can't do myself."

"I hope so," Randi said. "We're all they've got."

"Yeah, well, let's go get Maudie's stuff," Jared said.

"Only if I can hug you first," Randi said.

He didn't argue. And his arms were comforting as he pulled her in, though Randi noticed that he seemed to be almost quivering with the same excitement she was. "Is it always like this?" she asked.

"Only if you're lucky," he said. Then without another word he went for supplies and together they both went back to Crystal.

"That's a head!" Randi exclaimed a long time later. She hadn't looked at the clock in so long, she didn't know if it would be dawn soon or not. It felt like it ought to be noon instead. Her body hurt from bending, helping position Crystal, handing Jared things, and just feeling the tension of everything they were going through.

Crystal's pallor had changed to a flush, which deepened with each push that Jared was finally urging her on with. "That's great, Crystal. Randi's right. There's a head here. This baby has hair. Dark hair like Curtis. Looks like lots of it, too. One more good push and we can see what the face looks like. C'mon now."

Jared was frenetic, moving from Crystal's shoulder to encourage her, then down to the end of the bed where draped sheets were helping Randi provide a welcome place for the newest citizen of Redbud. Crystal gave an unearthly sound and Randi watched in wonder as the circle of head became a bluish-red face.

"Jared, what do I do now?"

"Nothing much, just get your hands ready to hold that baby. This is the hard part, Crystal. Is there a shoulder following, Miranda?"

"Yes. Whoa," she exclaimed as everything seemed to unfold at once.

"Okay then, get your hands ready. Support the head. Everything will happen real fast now. One more good push, Crystal." She made another sound Randi couldn't imagine coming out of a human being, and suddenly there, glistening in her hands, was a warm, squalling child.

"Well?" Crystal said. "Is everything okay?"

Randi was only then aware that there were tears running down her face as she looked down into the squashy face of the baby. "Just fine, I think." Her voice sounded distant and trembly.

"Stay solid there, Miranda," Jared urged her. He was beside her now, enveloping her and the baby. "Let me just wipe this little one's eyes and mouth a bit. Then we're going to rest her up on Mama for a while."

"Her?" Crystal reached out her arms. "Another girl?"

"And a beauty." Jared eased her down on a mass of pillows. "But we haven't cut the cord yet, so she can't go too far. Get comfy."

He settled the baby on Crystal's stomach and chest where her cries stilled to a soft mewing as her mother stroked her. Randi felt dazed watching all of it, knowing she'd helped a new life into the world.

"It's stopped pulsing." Jared's words broke in. "Why don't you cut it?"

"Me?"

"You. Tie off the way I showed you. That's right. Then just a snip. . ."

The next half hour or so passed in a haze. The baby nestled in Crystal's arms and she cautioned them again that she really didn't want to go to Park Hills to the hospital. "I mean, everything's all right, isn't it?"

"Couldn't be better," Jared told her, and seemed to Randi to mean it. There was an aura about him she'd never seen before, something of a wholeness and confidence that was almost uncanny.

Finally everything was cleaned up, and Randi realized it was dawn outside. "She was born on Christmas Eve," she said softly. "What are you going to call her?"

"Christine. I figure she'll probably be Tina later on. And none of that Noel stuff for a middle name, no matter when she was born." Crystal wrinkled her nose. "Christine Rebecca. That is, if you don't mind."

Rebecca—after her own little girl. Randi found herself misted with tears. "Not in the least."

"All right then. Try to sleep. Settle her in here when you get tired of counting her toes," Jared said, motioning to the bassinet they'd rigged up next to the bed. "We'll be in to check on you every so often."

He pulled Randi out in the hallway and they didn't get very far away before he was whirling her around with more vigor than Randi thought he would be capable of.

"You did it," she caroled.

"No, *we* did it, Miranda. And she's perfect and beautiful." He set her down and kissed her face in half a dozen places before he settled the sweetest kiss of all on her lips. "Thank you."

"I should be saying that to you, Jared. You got me through the scariest thing that's happened to me in years."

His cobalt eyes widened. "You were scared? Honey, you handled yourself like a pro."

"Only because of your coaching. But we did it. Isn't it wonderful?"

He squeezed her, hard. "It's more than wonderful. It's life changing. After this, anything I ever do again will be a breeze in comparison." He laughed, a full-throated sound that made Randi even more delighted than she was already.

"Now you go and get some rest, too," he said, kissing her again. "I'll take the first watch before you have to get up and function. Oh, Miranda, thank you so much for this. It makes everything else so right, and so simple."

"You're welcome," she said, even though she wasn't quite sure what Jared meant. Just to see him this happy was enough.

It seemed to take forever to scrub up, slip into clean sweats and fall into bed. Randi felt as if she'd died for a while and only came back to life when she became aware of a low whine near her ear. Bo had parked himself by the bed, tail thumping. When Randi poked her face out from under the pillows, he tilted his head and woofed a little, as if to urge her to get up and play.

"Right," she said. "Let me get lucid, okay?"

Bo stood up and shook as she slipped off the edge of the bed, stretching. He didn't seem to care what any other residents of the place were doing. Randi was his main concern. He took her wrist gently in his massive mouth and started walking her toward the door. She shook him off and made him follow her to the kitchen.

"You don't really have to get up and fix pancakes," Stevie told her when she got there. "I tried to tell that old dog several times not to go in and bother you, but he wouldn't listen."

"No, I usually fix a big breakfast on Saturdays and this is Christmas Eve. It is still Christmas Eve, isn't it?"

Stevie Joe laughed. "You didn't sleep that long. It's about noon."

Bo nosed Randi's hand again. "All right. Pancakes," she told him, rummaging for the ingredients. "How many am I fixing for?"

"I don't know if Crystal's up to eating yet. LoveAnne took her some juice awhile ago," Stevie said. Before

Randi could ask him if Jared was asleep somewhere, LoveAnne bounded into the room.

"Stevie? You really serious about the Miller place?" LoveAnne said, oblivious to anyone else in the room. "Because if you are, we better get over there before too long. You'll want to see it in daylight, and old man Miller, he's going to go to town for Christmas, I'm sure. Hi, Miss Randi."

LoveAnne stood near Stevie Joe and Randi looked from one to the other. "Mr. Nash? Anything you want to tell me?"

She didn't think anyone with that dark a tan could blush that spectacularly. "I do not. You all aren't the only ones who stayed up most of the night, though."

"We didn't do anything. Not anything wrong, anyway," LoveAnne said, lower lip pushed out petulantly. "The kids were bugging us to give them a ride in the bus, and we did and it put them to sleep and Asa stayed out in the bus with them while I took Stevie home. Then Daddy told him all about some places and then we all went out to see what they looked like in the moonlight. At least he and I did. Daddy went back to bed."

Ted Kimball had never been noted for keeping too close a hold on LoveAnne, but he wouldn't have let her go off all night with a man Stevie's age, either, unless things were on the up and up, Randi decided. There was something about the way the two looked at each other that told her that whatever had passed between them, it had been decided already.

"Well, all right. Just buying a farm, hmm?"

"Scout's honor. And I can show you my eagle merit badges," Stevie said. "Can you make pancakes?" he asked LoveAnne.

"Of course." Her voice was calm and almost condescending, even though Randi knew the lesson she'd given her a month before had been her first. "Randi and I will make breakfast. You just keep the children and that animal out of our way."

But Bo was not to be denied. He stopped tailing Randi and went over to LoveAnne, thrusting his head under her fingers until she had no choice but to scratch behind his ears. "Now go lie down and we'll bring you some," she told him mock sternly. He went.

"The queen is dead. Long live the queen," Randi muttered to herself, unable to keep a grin off her face. "Let's get to those pancakes," she told LoveAnne, looking at her to see if there were any traces of the young girl she knew left under the woman she'd grown into overnight.

Randi went back to the stove to see how LoveAnne was progressing. There was a huge stack of pancakes in the warming oven. "Almost done here," she said, smiling at Randi. "Then we can sit down. You think Stevie would shoot me if I gave Bo a plate of pancakes?"

"He'd probably choke," Randi said. "But the dog would be your friend for life."

"Good, because he got the first ones off the griddle," LoveAnne said with a giggle. There was an empty plate by the dog, who was stretched out in the corner with an expression of sleeping bliss on his jowly face. Randi stifled laughter, but only because she had no desire to explain the cause to any of the men sitting silently at the table.

"How long has Jared been asleep? Do you think I ought to wake him and give him some?"

LoveAnne looked up, seeming to calculate the time. "It's been at least a couple of hours. I bet he'd be hungry by now, if you wake him."

Randi wondered what shape Jared would be in. Only after she'd slipped into the darkened shelter room where he was sleeping did she stop to think about what he might or might not be wearing to sleep in.

He was fully clothed, stretched out on one of the cots with one hand dragging the floor. She sat on the floor beside him, softly kissing his stubbly cheek until he woke. "What?" he said, eyes open to slits.

"Oh, I bet you made a great resident, Jared Eden," she told him. "It's noon and there's a plate of pancakes with your name on them out there. Hungry?"

He rolled over on his side with a groan. "Starved. And in desperate need of a shower. Keep them warm for me a little while, will you?"

"With pleasure," Randi said. It was almost a Christmas gift to watch him wake up slowly. She wondered for a brief moment what it would be like to see that drowsy face on the next pillow every morning. No, not even Christmas would bring that kind of miracle.

Once Jared was up and stirring, everyone else cleared out of A Caring Place quickly. LoveAnne insisted on taking the entire crew to her house for Christmas, leaving only Crystal and the baby with her caretakers for the afternoon.

Jared was polishing off the last of his pancakes when Randi heard the baby cry. "Looks like somebody else is awake," he said with a smile.

She went to pick up the infant before Crystal could get out of bed. "I'll change her and get her all fixed up and bring her back," Randi told the new mother.

Now that she'd been bathed and slipped into a gown from the stores of clothing Randi kept on hand, Tina was beautiful. She had tons of fuzzy dark hair that haloed her little face. Two tiny clenched fists waved while Randi quickly diapered her, talking to her the whole time.

She marveled at the tiny perfection of the child. She had helped bring this little bundle into the world, and she was sound and healthy. Her lungs, Randi reflected, were particularly healthy.

"She's pinching you again, isn't she?" Jared came over to look down at Tina. As Randi picked her up off the bureau she was using for a changing table, Jared scooped his large hands under her and brought her up between them. "Now what's all the racket about?"

His gentle, deep voice stilled the baby's crying. She hiccuped a little while she opened her eyes wider than Randi had seen them open before to stare at the man who held her. Randi wondered what she saw. She knew most people said newborns couldn't see very well. It would be a shame if Tina couldn't see the look of utter bemusement on Jared's face as he looked down at her.

She squirmed a little after a moment, and her face puckered up. "Better get you in to see Mom," Jared said. "I certainly can't provide what you're looking for." Randi watched him walk down the hall, perfectly at ease carrying the tiny baby. He'd surprised her again.

She gathered the blanket that Tina had been wrapped in. It was damp. Might as well add it to the mountain of laundry their night-long adventure had left.

While she folded clothes, she let herself daydream about what things could be like if Jared stayed, *really* stayed this time. With the money coming in, maybe they could make a real clinic, even almost a minihospital out of A Caring Place.

Then eventually Maudie could retire to go live with her sister in Hot Springs like she always said she would. They would buy her house when they bought the practice, and folks would come and bang on the door in the middle of the night for Doc Tarkett.

Her reverie was interrupted by a large, wet-haired male nuzzling the back of her neck. "You're cold," she told him.

"Not at all. Just my wet hair," he answered, nuzzling in even closer. "The rest of me is very warm."

"This is true," she murmured. And the warmth pushed all her daydreams to the background as she concentrated on the very real present being in Jared's arms.

Jared woke up on Christmas Day wondering what he was going to do. Part of the answer was easy. But here he was, empty-handed, when he wanted to give Miranda something special. So special that she'd know how much she meant to him.

It would take some planning. And leaving again. She was going to have a conniption fit about that one, but it couldn't be helped. He tried to keep that thought out of his mind while they had breakfast together with Stevie Joe and his awful dog and Crystal, who got up and dressed and came to the table for the first time.

Randi looked gorgeous even if she wasn't wearing anything fancier than a Christmas sweater and jeans. She apologized for her lack of presents. "We'll go out and get something together soon," she told him. It was hard to agree, knowing what he was going to do, instead. But it was easier than telling her the truth and spoiling her Christmas morning.

The rest of Christmas Day Jared had little time to wonder what he was going to do next. LoveAnne and her father insisted on making things a holiday for everyone holed up at A Caring Place, and Randi didn't argue.

So they helped settle Crystal in the bus with Tina, in a brand-new car seat from Stevie, who carefully transported the entire crew to the Kimballs' for turkey.

Even Bo sat under the table, and after dinner he wandered out to let the children maul him. He sat good-naturedly while Curtis pondered how to ride him like a horse, and let Lindy chatter to him incessantly when she wasn't hopping on and off Jared's lap.

This was the first time Christmas had felt like a family day in years, he pondered. And he wasn't even with his family. Not his birth family, anyway. He had an idea that if he stayed around this part of the country, his definition of family was going to be a whole lot different in times to come.

Randi watched Jared ease Lindy off his lap again so she could go batter the dog. He looked slightly edgy, as if he were tired of being indoors. Surely he wasn't going to get on that bike on Christmas Day? She pushed the thought out of mind and helped LoveAnne clear the table.

"Don't be doing this after today," Randi cautioned LoveAnne as they did the dishes together in the kitchen. "I know you have homework to catch up on. You will graduate on time," she admonished.

"Nothing would keep me from it," the young woman told her, leaving Randi again to wonder what had happened overnight.

At the supper table, Stevie Joe was telling Ted and Crystal all about the Miller farm that would be his come Monday.

"It's the kind of place I didn't even know I needed until I saw it," he said. "Get me out of all that city glitz in Nashville and back to clean air. I should have another album worth of songs in no time."

"You always have another album worth of songs in no time," Asa said. "I suppose we'll have to suffer through a whole bunch of 'back to nature' tracks on this one."

Faced by their good-natured gibes, he laughed, and Jared laughed with him. It felt good, knowing that he was happy and content. She tried to tell herself that everything had worked out for the best, but no matter how many times she said it in her mind, she couldn't quite believe it.

"You're going to leave again, aren't you?" The question seemed to startle Jared. He turned to Randi where they were both sitting on the battered couch in one of the classrooms. Everyone else was tucked up for the night and they'd been sitting together in the darkened room, watching the stars come out on the other side of the window glass.

He looked at her, blue eyes clouded with sudden pain. "Yes. But I'll be back. I promise, Miranda. There's just something I have to do."

She felt herself stiffen with his arm around her. "Then go and do it, Jared. But don't expect me to be happy about your going."

"I'll come back."

"Will you?" It was hard to keep her voice at a normal level. Her miracle Christmas was disintegrating in front of her and Randi wanted to scream.

"I will. Give me two days, all right? Just two."

"I'll give you anything you need, Jared. Willingly. But you know that making me watch you leave is the hardest thing you can do to me."

He was standing then, looking out the window. "So don't watch. Want me to get going early in the morning so you don't have to face me?"

"Maybe that would be best," Randi found herself saying. "Good night." She left the room before Jared could turn and say anything, or try to touch her. Right now she didn't want his touch. It would only be a reminder that it wouldn't last.

In the morning when she woke, Randi knew instantly that he was already gone. The building was still full of sounds. There was the hum of the new furnace, making all the rooms toasty. There was the click of Bo pacing outside her door.

Somewhere down the hall Tina was awake and hollering while Crystal changed her and got her ready for her breakfast. Stevie had apparently come in and started something in the kitchen because a country music station played softly on the radio.

But there was an emptiness to the sound that told her the one person she really cared to hear in the morning was gone. Jared was already on his bike, bound for Denton, Texas. She knew that's where he was, and she wondered how soon he'd be surprising his family by coming back to the fold.

There was no doubt in her mind that that was what was happening. He'd hinted at it himself, thanking her, telling her how easy it would be for him, now that he knew his medical skills were still there. Of course he'd go back to being a doctor. And it was only natural that he'd want to do it at home.

She wondered if he would call. And what she would say when he did. It was then the tears came, so hard that she had to burrow into her pillow.

Randi had wished for a miracle, and she'd gotten more than one. There had been Jared in the first place, and everything that went with him.

Now Jared was well and confident, Crystal had a beautiful baby and Randi had more problems than she'd ever had before. She'd been given the greatest gift she'd ever received from anyone, but he hadn't stayed around to watch it blossom into reality.

All of her love for Jared seemed to be disintegrating in the face of this abandonment. Her mind was flooded with the memories of all the other people who'd walked out on her, broken their promises, left without explanation. Because this time, despite his protest, she was so afraid he wasn't coming back.

Chapter Ten

Three days after Christmas Randi woke up totally alone. It was jarring to look around the bright, shining building and see it conversely filled with shattered dreams.

Somehow Stevie and Bo had known enough to stay out of her way most of the time once Jared was gone. There were phone calls to make Monday morning, and the usual paperwork to plow through, Crystal to take care of and the children darting in and out of the office.

LoveAnne had come in midafternoon to take the children for a few hours, just to get them out of everyone's hair. When she brought them back, she was waving a piece of paper. "Got a nice surprise in the mail. First semester grades. All A's and a B in biology, just like I told you."

"Keep them going, sugar," Randi said, standing up from her desk.

"I have to," LoveAnne said, oblivious to Randi's worry. "I don't have any choice."

"I'm glad you still see it that way." Randi crossed the office to where LoveAnne stood in the doorway with the computer printout of her grades. "Some less mature people would be considering a career as a groupie right now."

LoveAnne tossed her head. "Like I'd want to be on that bus with that old dog. No, sir. I need that education worse than ever now. Stevie may want to live in Redbud, but he doesn't want his children growing up ignorant."

"Children?" Randi's hands went automatically to the girl's slim shoulders. "What are you trying to tell me?"

"Not what you think, Randi." The eyes that looked back at her were calm, no longer dreamy. "I just know, is all. Not now, but when the time is right. It will happen."

It would, too, if the self-assured person in front of her had anything to say about it, Randi thought. "Okay, sweetie. You just scared me, is all."

A giggle escaped when LoveAnne gently took Randi's hands off her shoulders. "Don't worry. Sometimes the last few days, I've scared myself."

It was the last said about the matter before Stevie pulled into the lot and came out waving all his deeds and papers proving him the proud owner of a piece of ground, a falling-down barn and a white house in need of paint. It all seemed to thrill him silly. Bo had caught his infectious delight and was bouncing at his heels. LoveAnne hugged Stevie first and then the dog, and then went back to Stevie, who picked her up and whirled her around once before setting her down.

He'd insisted on getting burgers for everyone from the drive-in in Park Hills by way of celebration. "What does Bo like on his hamburgers?" Randi teased.

"Barbecue sauce and onions," Stevie and LoveAnne chorused. Randi wrinkled her nose and grabbed the jowly face at her knee.

"You can sit in the gym, but you aren't sleeping in my room tonight. Not .after eating onions, sport." He seemed to sigh as she let him into the car.

Tuesday morning, Stevie and Bo and Asa stayed out at the farm, so Stevie could show it off before he left it for a month. Tuesday afternoon he used the bus to transport Crystal and her family back to their house at her insistence.

"We've got to start doing this on our own sometime," she told Randi. "You've done so much already."

Randi had tried to argue her into staying a few more days. The weather was changing and there was definitely going to be snow. There had been no calls from Jared and she was worried about him.

Half the time she could convince herself that he was coming back. He was doing just fine, just not bothering to call, and this evening she'd hear the thrum of an engine and there he would be, tires kicking up gravel in the parking lot. Then she started worrying about the weather, until she told herself it just wouldn't do to fret herself into a wreck.

When Stevie came back from taking Crystal home, it was time for him to leave. He and LoveAnne had obviously already said their goodbyes somewhere else, and now it was time to say goodbye to Randi.

"I know it's dumb, buying this place here, as much as I'm on the road," he told Randi. "But it's time for my own place like this again. I'll be back." He meant it, too, she discovered in the depths of his eyes. She didn't know who to feel sorrier for, him or LoveAnne. Both seemed to have their work cut out for them for years to come.

Her own future was a whole lot less certain and Stevie seemed to sense her aching. "He'll be back. Or he'll call. Soon. I'm just positive."

"It can't be soon enough," Randi told him. "You drive careful in the weather, you hear? Pull off the road if it gets bad."

"Don't worry. We always take extra time just to keep out of bad situations," Stevie said. Then he and Asa climbed aboard the bus and were gone. She waved when he drove off, and then went back inside to face the empty building alone.

In an hour it was snowing, hard. An hour after that the wind picked up and the twilight turned to dark in what seemed to be a split second. Randi knew she was going to spend the night looking out the window, watching and wondering about Jared. She was a fool for letting him go anywhere.

In the light in the morning it wasn't any better. Randi was still alone in the echoing building. The snow had piled up all night until there were drifts even with the front porch steps. Picking up the phone in the office to call and make sure Crystal was all right only proved that the phone lines were out.

Randi put the receiver down in aggravation and started pacing the building, looking for something to do. Finally she settled on more laundry while she still had electricity. There was all of the flotsam left from several more days of taking care of Crystal and Tina.

She looked around the place, feeling cross. Maudie should be back soon from Arkansas, and Randi was sorry about what she was going to be telling her. There were always budget cuts, cash shortages, plenty of sick people, but no help except herself. "And we all know what that's worth," she muttered, stripping the sheets off Jared's bed.

"Why didn't you stay?" she asked the light scent of him that still clung to the room. "I needed you around here to take care of me." Still standing in Jared's room, hugging the bundle of sheets to her chest, Randi froze. Her head was reeling with the implication of what she'd just told herself. Was that really what she needed from Jared? A big, strong man to come and take over her life?

She was swamped by feelings as she sat on the edge of the stripped bed. She'd held an image of him in her mind all these weeks, of his being her white knight, the town's white knight. Riding in on his motorcycle charger and making everything right.

But from the first, that wasn't what he'd really done. He'd come bruised and battered, needing to be healed. He'd kissed her hand in gratitude for a glass of cold water. And he'd made her feel more like a woman, and a satisfied human being, than anyone else ever had before he'd ever fixed anything.

None of her happiness had come about because he was trying to take over. In fact, the greatest happiness of all came when he was making her do what he convinced her she could do by herself. The sheets slid to the floor as Randi walked out of the room, feeling a little like LoveAnne must in her teenage dazes. Jared had made her feel whole by demanding she act like a whole person. Jared had made her solve her own problems, fight her own battles, stepping in only when he could provide something she just didn't have.

Yes, of course she needed Jared. Just as much as he needed her. They both had dreams to accomplish. But it wasn't right to demand that he accomplish hers any more than it would be for him to make her live whatever plans he'd made after their long night delivering Tina. Laundry forgotten for once, Randi knew what she had to do.

Hours later when she stopped for breath, Randi reflected on what Stevie Joe had said. Jared would be back. And she'd be there waiting for him, if she hadn't worried herself to a nub wondering where he was in this weather. It was what she deserved, anyway. She'd counted too much on Jared for the wrong reasons. It galled her that the perfect man had fallen into her lap, or at least in her front yard, and all she could see while he was there was that he had mowed down her Christmas tree.

What he was, what he'd been all along, was her miracle. Not a miracle by coming in and fixing everything. No, a miracle for just being Jared.

He'd made her look inside herself and see what was still there worth salvaging. He'd showed her that she could do whatever she set out to do, even delivering a beautiful, healthy baby like Tina. And then he'd left and she hadn't even told him goodbye.

"That wasn't fair," she told Jared, even though he was someplace where he couldn't hear her. She just hoped that the phone lines would come back soon. There was so much she needed to do and all it took was a telephone. First on the list was a call to Denton, Texas.

She couldn't make the call until Friday morning when the phone lines finally came back. Jared still hadn't shown up. Randi was beginning to wonder whether to hug him or strangle him when he got back, for giving her gray hair.

The call to Denton didn't help the decision any. The nice receptionist at Tarkett Clinic was firm, friendly but not enlightening. No, young Dr. Tarkett sure hadn't come back to town. She believed they'd heard from him in the past few days, but he wasn't in Denton. Not yet, anyway.

"So where are you?" Randi said, glaring at the phone receiver with its dial tone. Maybe she should call Carl and see what kind of checks they should be making of hospitals and such. And the state highway patrol. Why did the man go gallivanting off in the middle of the winter on a motorcycle?

Because he was Jared, she told herself. It brought such a quirky smile to her face to think about him and his stubborn, obnoxious and endearing ways that she couldn't believe he wasn't here to share it.

And in that moment he was, not just in spirit, but in the roar of that bike out front and gravel spewing in the lot.

She was out the door in a flash and down the stairs just about the time he had put both feet on the ground and slipped off his helmet.

"Whoa," he said as she plowed into him. "I didn't think I'd get this kind of welcome, being gone as long as I was."

"You're back," she said, looking up at his dark hair and sparkling eyes. "And apparently in one piece." It was still snowing outside, hard, and Randi had dashed outside without her coat. But at the moment she was too happy and relieved to notice.

"Yeah. One piece that's kind of cold and sore. Remind me to get something more comfortable for snow than this bike. If I'm going to stay up here where the weather is this lousy, I've got to get a vehicle with a roof."

"I'll make sure you do," Randi said, unwilling to let go of him for even an instant. He hugged her back, tighter, and laughed.

"You're really not going to kill me, are you?" he asked.

"Not now, that you're finally here. I was terribly worried, though, Jared."

His face got more serious. "I know. I figured you would be. But at first I thought I could get everything done and be back. And then it started snowing, and about the time I talked myself out of staying on the road, the phone lines must have gone down here."

"Let's go inside, and you can warm up and tell me all about it," Randi said.

He bent down and kissed her. At first his lips were cold but the core of him was warm and she was able to forget the cold wind and the snow and tangle her fingers in the dark silk of his hair and enjoy welcoming him back. Then he grabbed a box from the back of his bike, put his free arm around Randi, and accompanied her up the stairs and into the building.

"Now," Randi said, comfortably settling into his lap. Jared had a cup of coffee and was beginning to thaw out, and she couldn't get close enough to him. "What was so important that it couldn't wait until later? Until I called them, I thought maybe you'd gone back to Texas."

Jared looked surprised. "Nothing that important there, Miranda. I did call home to tell them where I am and wish them a Merry Christmas." His father had been stunned, too. "But when I go back there, it will be with you. They want to meet you."

"And eventually I want to meet them. But there's so much to deal with first. Like the ad I've already paid to place in the Sunday St. Louis papers to hire someone to replace me.''

Jared went from looking surprised to stunned. ''You're quitting? But I thought this was your life. Lord, have I made a terrible mistake being gone this long?''

''I hope not. As antsy as you've been so far to travel, I didn't figure you'd mind leaving a one-horse town like this, at least for a while. My only problem is how to pay this person if I hire somebody.''

''Don't worry about that,'' Jared said softly, pulling her even closer. ''Hell, I'll have money till the cows come home, Miranda.'' It was true. And he couldn't think of a way he'd rather spend it, except maybe what he'd been doing for the past few days. She looked down into his face. Jared knew everything was going to be all right when her expression softened and she traced with her fingers the spot he knew she still half wanted to smack for giving her so much trouble.

''I shouldn't let you off so easy. Jared, you took off with no explanation. Leaving me stranded just after Christmas.''

''Only because I knew what I wanted to do. What we should do together. And I thought you knew...''

''Well, I didn't,'' she said, looking as if she was going to cry.

He couldn't stand that. ''Please don't do that. I want to make you happy. How about we start with this?''

Randi looked at the box in her hands. It was the one he'd taken off the back of the bike when he came in. ''It rattles,'' she said hopefully.

''Open it before I lose what little of my composure is left,'' Jared warned. She complied, tearing open the cardboard like a kid. The box inside, wrapped in red foil, slowed her down a little. Silently he urged her to open that one as well.

Finally she got to the small velvet box nestled inside. Her eyes really filled with tears this time, and she seemed speechless. Jared filled the silence. "I want to spend the rest of my life with you. No more running away. I love you, Miranda, and I'm going to marry you, if you'll have me."

Miranda blinked back her tears. "Have you? Nobody could make me let go of you, Jared Tarkett."

"I was so afraid you'd say no. I know you've been married before and it was no walk in the park."

"It wasn't with the right person," Miranda said simply. "I love you, Jared. This ring, and what it means, is the most wonderful surprise I could have gotten for Christmas."

"I wanted something fitting." He looked at the box in her hand. "There aren't many jewelers open in Columbia and I spent most of my time trying to get you an interview at the med school anyway. But you like the ring?"

"It's beautiful. You put it on." He slipped it on her hand and kissed the palm. Her expression told him they were both thinking of the same thing, that night that seemed ages ago when he'd kissed her hand the first time.

For a while neither of them spoke. When Randi did, it was going back to a comment he'd thought she hadn't heard. "Do I really have an interview at the med school?"

Jared kissed her again. "You sure do. I managed to pull a whole bunch of strings. Set myself up to begin an MBA so I can manage this medical practice once you get out, and got you in with the medical school review board. Of course, the fact that your transcript was in order and the application half filled out in your desk drawer didn't hurt.'' He pulled his head back, looking at her hard as he had a disturbing thought. ''What's the matter? Did you already set up an interview yourself?''

She leaned her forehead against his chest, laughing softly as she wrapped her hands around his shoulders. ''No. Even I don't move that fast.''

He leaned into her, cradling her body with his. The welcome scent of her, sunshine and wildflowers, filled him. ''I really meant to get back here before that snow.''

''It would have been more convenient,'' Randi said into his chest. ''Oh, Jared, I love you so much. Why did you have to go and do something goofy like this, just when I was ready to do it all myself?''

He had to swallow hard before he answered, unable yet to let go of her. ''Because I love you, too. You gave me back a life, Miranda. The least I could do was give you one in return.''

''You will, Jared.'' She looked up with shining eyes. ''You already have. And someday, when we're through building these dreams, we'll make another life. One that isn't yours and isn't mine, but is ours to share.''

''And that we will definitely plan together.''

''But we've got so many other things to plan first,'' she said before his lips met hers. ''And you can forget waiting until Columbia for that justice of the peace. We aren't going anyplace else until I hear you make some promises I know you aim to keep.''

Jared threw back his head for a laugh. It felt good, almost as good as the woman in his arms. ''My practical Miranda. Fine. Wherever we go, we'll be together.''

''Good. I don't intend to do any more traveling tonight, though.''

Jared was about to ask why not, when it dawned on him. "It's New Year's Eve. Not a great night for traveling, I guess."

"More like a time for plans and resolutions," she said, kissing him. "Tomorrow we can travel, all the way to the bus station in Park Hills. Maudie comes back then. Heck, if we get our plans far enough, maybe she'll even be a witness. I'll bet Carl knows the quickest way to get a license." It was all Randi got out before Jared kissed her into silence.

He was the one who broke the silence finally, pulling away and groaning. "Oh, Lord. I'm going to spend my honeymoon in a grade school."

"At least it won't be in one of those cots," Randi teased.

Jared wanted to see if he could make her blush. "I don't know. It bears thinking about. There might be some interesting possibilities there."

She turned an interesting shade of pink and tugged his forelock. "You're incorrigible."

"Would you want it any other way?"

"Never. Looks like I got my miracle after all."

"I don't know about being anybody's miracle. But I'm here to stay. As long as you want me, Miranda." He didn't realize he was holding his breath until she answered.

"I sure do want you," she said. "For longer than you can imagine."

"I've got a very vivid imagination," he said.

"We'll just see, Jared Eden, how vivid it is."

It was vivid enough to imagine miracles, Miranda knew that. And here, in Jared's arms, she could imagine them, as well. Lots of them, more than she could ever ask for. Starting now, she was going to stop asking for miracles. It looked like she had all she could handle for a lifetime.

Epilogue

Sleet hissed on the tin roof of the big brick house and Randi snuggled into the nest of quilts on the brass bed. The noise that was disturbing her sleep was a familiar one, and it was all too real.

The thumping on the door just wasn't going to stop until she put on a robe and went down and answered it. Whoever was there had plenty of energy. From the stairway it sounded like the heavy oak door was about to come off its hinges. "Doc? Doc Tarkett?"

Oh, Lord. It was Stevie Ray. Miranda made it down the last of the stairs and unlocked the door. "Stevie? What are you doing out in this weather?"

"It's time," he said grimly. There were little ice drips on the edges of his dark hat. "LoveAnne told me she thought it was, and I told her it was just nerves. Hell, we've been up here to your hospital three times and every time y'all've sent us back home. So I told her just to hold on, and now she says it's really time. You're going to have to come out there with me, Doc. I didn't dare try to bump her down those gravel roads to get her here."

Randi sighed. "I expect I better go, then. You did bring the 4 × 4, didn't you? And there's somebody with her?"

"Loralee came for supper and stayed the night." There was real panic in his green eyes. "How could I be this dense? And how come she let me?"

"Because she loves you and you listen poorly. Wait here. Call her if you want while I get my things together."

Randi went back up the stairs while the nervous father fumbled with her telephone in the downstairs hall. When she switched the light on in the bedroom, a huge black mound rose from the foot of the bed.

"Oh, lie down," she told the Newfoundland. "Stevie hasn't got room for you in there."

"He's used to tagging along," Jared said from the doorway. "LoveAnne?"

"Yes." Randi zipped up the jeans that were lying on the chair next to the bed, and began twisting her hair back. "You going to be all right here?"

"We'll be fine." Jared patted the rump of the small bundle balanced on his naked chest. "Tell Mama we'll just sit in the rocker and play until she gets back, Miss Katherine."

"Oh, Jared. Three-month-olds don't talk, even precocious ones like Katydid. And you ought to put her back in the crib or she'll get to thinking three in the morning is playtime."

"It is for some of us," he said with a devilish smile. "We'll be good, I promise. Now go catch her a playmate, okay?"

She came over to kiss the both of them, reveling in the warm smell of baby and husband all wrapped up into one. "I'll do that." The dog wasn't to be put off from going with her, and as Randi grabbed her medical bag he stood beside her, ready to go downstairs.

"Oh, come on then. No one in this family has the sense to stay out of bad weather," she told the dog. "You might as well fit in." The big dog padded down the stairs with her, out the door and into the 4×4 that Stevie Ray had ready to shoot down the road for the farm where another new life was ready to come into the world.

Looking up, Randi could see one faint light on upstairs, gleaming through the sleet-iced window. Her traveling man had traveled as far as the nursery again. These days it seemed all the journey he needed. Here were her miracles on top of miracles...Jared, Katie, her practice. It was all almost too miraculous to be true. The truck lurched into gear and the dog leaned against her. "Now tell me, what's going on at home?" she prompted Stevie.

"She started having contractions about ten, and we thought it was those Braxton things again. Or at least I did. So I said it was no sense bothering you a third time until something really happened. Then something really did. I think we're going to have to burn that mattress."

Randi leaned against the furry mountain of her dog. It was going to be another long night for the doctor in the Tarkett household. But when she came home in the morning, there would be Jared and Katherine waiting for her. "I bet he'll make us pancakes," she whispered to the dog. He moaned in happiness and settled down beside her while she settled herself more securely in the seat of the bouncing truck.

*   *   *   *   *

MILLION DOLLAR SWEEPSTAKES (III)

Montana Mavericks ™

Stories that capture living and loving
beneath the Big Sky, where legends live
on...and mystery lingers.

This December, explore more MONTANA MAVERICKS with

THE RANCHER TAKES A WIFE
by Jackie Merritt

He'd made up his mind. He'd loved her almost a lifetime
and now he was going to have her, come hell or high
water.

And don't miss a minute of the loving as the passion continues with:

OUTLAW LOVERS
by Pat Warren (January)

WAY OF THE WOLF
by Rebecca Daniels (February)

THE LAW IS NO LADY
by Helen R. Myers (March)
and many more!

Only from *Silhouette*® where passion lives.

HE'S MORE THAN A MAN,
HE'S ONE OF OUR

IDEAL DAD
Elizabeth August

Eight-year-old Jeremy Galvin knew Murdock Parnell would make the perfect dad. Now it was up to Murdock to persuade Jeremy's mom, Irene, that he was the ideal husband for her.

Ideal Dad, available in January, is the third book in Elizabeth August's bestselling series, WHERE THE HEART IS.

Look for *Ideal Dad* by Elizabeth August—available in January.

Fall in love with our Fabulous Fathers!

Silhouette
R O M A N C E™

Silhouette ROMANCE™

BELIEVING IN MIRACLES
by
Linda Varner

Carpenter Andy Fulbright and Honorine "Honey" Truman had all the criteria for a perfect marriage—they liked and respected each other, they desired and needed each other...and *neither* one loved the other! But with the help of some mistletoe and two young elves, these two might learn to believe in the miracle of Christmas....

BELIEVING IN MIRACLES is the second book in Linda Varner's MR. RIGHT, INC., a heartwarming series about three hardworking bachelors in the building trade who find love at first sight—construction site, that is!

Don't miss BELIEVING IN MIRACLES, available in December. And look for Book 3, WIFE MOST UNLIKELY, in March 1995. Read along as old friends make the difficult transition to lovers....

Only from *Silhouette*®

where passion lives.

Those Harris boys are back in book three of...

WEDDING WAGER

by Sandra Steffen

Three sexy, single brothers bet they'll never say "I do."
But the Harris boys are about to discover their vows of bachelor-hood don't stand a chance against the forces of love!

You met Mitch in BACHELOR DADDY #1028 (8/94) and Kyle in BACHELOR AT THE WEDDING #1045 (11/94). Now it's time for brother Taylor to take the marriage plunge in—

EXPECTANT BACHELOR #1056 (1/95): When Gina Jenson sets out to seduce the handsome Taylor, he's in for the surprise of his life. Because Gina wants him to father her child!
